On the run

Tamar put her hand to her mouth, closed her eyes briefly, then shrugged. "Might as well tell you, now you've noticed them. It's a handbill about a runaway slave. The reward for him is three hundred dollars."

"Dat's lotsa dollahs."

"There's been more offered for us." She spoke, then stiffened as though wishing to recover the words.

"Dey got—han'bills 'bout *we*, Aunty?" I said, my heart dropping toewards.

Tamar blew out a breath. "Yes. I saw several, a long way back, and tore them down before you noticed."

"What dey say 'bout we? How much we count fer?"

"A thousand dollars for me, five hundred for you. The posters said that I'm an unusually tall, bad-tempered, dark-complected woman, good cook, about thirty years old, and that you are a small boy about ten or eleven, lightish skin and good with horses. That we are probably together."

I swallowed hard, looked again at the little running black person on the handbill. "You t'ink dey mought could cotch we dis far fum de plantation, Aunty?"

"I think we'd better get back in the woods. Stay off the roads altogether."

CEZANNE PINTO

Other Knopf Paperbacks you will enjoy:

CEZANNE PINTO

A MEMOIR

MARY STOLZ

A KNOPF PAPERBACK

Alfred A. Knopf · New York

For Robert O. Warren

A KNOPF PAPERBACK PUBLISHED BY ALFRED A. KNOPF, INC.

Text copyright © 1994 by Mary Stolz
Cover art copyright © 1994 by Jane Sterrett

//www.randomhouse.com/

Library of Congress Cataloging-in-Publication Data
Stolz, Mary.
Cezanne Pinto / by Mary Stolz.
p.   cm.
Summary: In his old age Cezanne Pinto recalls his youth as a slave on a Virginia
plantation and his escape to a new life in the North.
[1. Slavery—Fiction. 2. Afro-Americans—Fiction. 3. Underground railroad—Fiction.] I. Title.
PZ7.S875854Ce   1994
[Fic]—dc20
92-46765

ISBN 0-679-84917-3 (trade)
ISBN 0-679-88933-7 (pbk.)

First Knopf Paperback edition: December 1997
Printed in the United States of America
10 9 8 7 6 5 4 3 2

A Memoir

---

by Cezanne Pinto

dedicated to my ancestors and to my descendants

CHAPTER ONE

In 1860, when I ran from the plantation in Virginia, I decided to be twelve years old. Could've been anywhere from nine to fourteen, but as Frederick Douglass, that great man, said, you might as well ask a horse how old he is as a slave.

Twelve sounded all right to me, then. Now my beaky nose is pushing the ninety mark (or past it, who knows?) and one day follows another day like one boxcar coupled to another boxcar, all of them back of an engine going nowhere. This is an observation, not a complaint. I have had a life crammed with love, labor, exhilaration, exhaustion, rage, pain, pleasure.

And now?

Now I say, "Enough!"

I'll be fine on this siding the rest of the way, and

will use up the time filling a school notebook with recollections of how it felt to be me . . .

I will tell you about my mother.

We slave children were obliged to call our mothers "Mammy." "Mother," even "Mama"—those were white words, and in front of white folks we said "Mammy" or got whipped.

But my mother said to call her "Mam" when we were alone. Years later I learned that English queens are addressed as "Ma'am." *There's* something to think about.

Mam was queenly.

African queenly.

Quiet and quick as a slim dark cat, she had the wonderful gait all slave women developed early from carrying bundles atop their heads. She was cook in the Big House of the plantation where I was born. It was called Gloriana, after an English queen.

The state of Virginia was named for the same queen, which is the sort of unimportant interesting fact that I enjoy knowing.

*   *   *

Looking back, I realize that like many of those Dixieland domains, Gloriana was showy and shoddy. The horses were excellent, and well tended, but the plantation carriages were fancy rigs with peeling paint, and the Big House was like a once elegant woman turned sloven. The Clayburns—master and mistress and daughters three—were indolent lords of their manor. Though the place was *stuffed* with black house servants, headed by a self-important butler named Herkimer, nothing was well taken care of . . . their fancy, furbelowed clothes not really clean, silver and brass not properly polished, crystal chandeliers and glasses faintly smeary.

As Mam said, why keep a place well, or care about it, for people who didn't know what well kept or cared for was?—not for furniture, for chandeliers, or for breathing, suffering human beings.

Outside was a different matter.

Stables and barns, corn and tobacco fields, orchards, and the slave quarter were run by a white overseer, name of Blade. He was known as a man who could "handle" us. *Us* being the breathing, suf-

5

fering human beings at his mercy. Deaf to pleas or pity, suspicious that we might know a moment of peace, even—unlikely as that might be—of pleasure, if he relaxed the scrutiny of his blue, pale, angry eyes, Blade drove us to exhaustion, drove many to run, to escape the absolute rule of his blacksnake whip.

Some of us, defeated in spirit and body, knocked at Death's door, and were kindly taken in.

Blade cheated Clayburn left, right, all around the barn. We knew that, and it was the only thing about him any of us commended. We didn't like "Ol' Massa," but that was just practice for how we felt about Blade, whose vicious ways were surely among the reasons Ol' Massa fell on hard times, so that he took to selling slaves. (Sometimes he hired them out to neighbors. A sort of nineteenth-century rent-a-slave deal.) One year he sold several, including my mother, to a cattleman from Texas. Mam fetched a good price, being known as the best cook for miles in any direction.

She *begged*, got on her *knees*—not a woman to be brought to her knees any other way—to have me bought along with her. Except for my older sister, who'd been sold to a slave trader years before, I was all the child she had. Gone too, so long before I couldn't call to mind his face, was the man who was my father.

But no—the Texas cattleman said he only needed ranch hands and a cook, he had too many useless slave children already, and besides, I had a look in my eye he didn't rightly take to.

I recall how Clayburn told the Texan, "That there boy's daddy was mean as a badger. Made a reg'lar habit of runnin' off. Even my overseer, Blade, couldn't flog him into shape. Finally sent him to a slave breaker, and damned if he didn't beat the breaker up and run off again. Sent the patty-rollers after him, but they never catched sight of even his shadder."

Clayburn was not a well-spoken man, in any sense.

Patty-rollers? Well, how could you know? I'll *tell* you, though. Patty-rollers (patrollers) were slave hunters, slave thrashers, slave entrappers. They prowled by night looking for runaways that they'd return, in leg irons and neck collars, to their owners. Patty-rollers stopped honest black folk coming late from church or a visit to a relative a few miles off, because we were not supposed to be out of our own slave quarters after dark.

When possible, these dread sentries took free black men and women, those who had proper passes to prove they were not slaves, and sold them "down the river."

Down the Mississippi.

There, in Deep South states, no one listened to a black person explaining how he was "free"—"See, *looka yere!* He had this paper *proving* how he was a free man." They'd laugh at his claim, tear up the pass, and it was back into bondage for him, who had maybe risked death to escape it.

Not so many women as men escaped Southern fields and manor houses, because of not wanting either to leave their children or to take them on risk-ridden flights. Some took the mighty chance, and Harriet Tubman—the great, the glorious, and defiant, heroic, matchless Harriet, called "Moses" by her people—led many a man, woman, and child to freedom.

Out of the Egypt of Dixie into the Promised Land.

My father was sold to Clayburn by his first master because of this habit he had of escaping. Until that last time, they always caught him. Brought him "home" in irons. He might have been a difficult property to dispose of, but he was an ideal slave—huge and strong, young and illiterate. He was intelligent, too, but the seller hadn't warned Clayburn of that.

Cupid, the blacksmith, told me how Ol' Massa had said to Blade, "I snapped up this here new one at a bargain, but he's surly and got the devil's own temper. I'm relyin' on you to knock him into shape."

Blade had knocked many an unruly bargain into shape, but not one like my father. However, what Blade couldn't do, one look at Mam achieved. She slowed him to a walk, kept him enslaved, in all senses, for years.

"How we was in love in love in love," she'd tell me. "I was sixteen, thereabouts, and purty as a pitcher iffen I do say so. And your daddy, Deucy, your daddy was such a man—such a man—like no man in the worl' else. The secon' I clapped eyes on him, my heart lep' into his han' like a baby rabbit 'n' nestled dere snug as snug. We had a broomstick weddin', and we was happy. For a while we was happy, for a while, for a while, for a sometime while . . ."

Mam had a way of repeating a phrase so that it sounded like a clock chiming, a bell pealing—or tolling . . .

They were wed, my pretty mother, my big strong intelligent unread unmanageable father.

When slaves married?

The couple jumped over a broomstick.

That completed the ceremony.

"When y'all done cleared this yere broomstick, y'all married," the white preacher, the overseer, now and then the master, would say. "Now get back to work."

You think I exaggerate? I do not exaggerate. I state a fact.

I tell you further, a slave could not defend his family against beatings, auctions, shameful behavior on the part of owners. When such things happened—and they happened all the time, all the time—a slave man had three choices. To stand by and do nothing, to fight and get flogged, to run away. A slave had no more legal standing than a—a horse, as Frederick Douglass put it again and again.

Mam told me how when Sister was sold to the slave

trader, my daddy knocked Blade senseless one night and ran off to the North, to New York State, where he got a job in a shipyard. Then he staked all—his freedom, his life—to return weeks later to the quarter. Tried to coax Mam to come along with him, run to the North. I was too little to take along and she wouldn't leave me. He went on by himself.

He said he'd work to buy her freedom, and mine, but we never heard of him again. I try to believe he made it to freedom but couldn't earn enough money to buy us. I don't want to think of other ends he might have met, other ways he was kept from coming for us.

And Mam. My mother. I hope she found something to live for, after the war was over, maybe even found a measure of happiness.

I'll tell now how I got my name, Cezanne Pinto.

First, I should explain that my slave name was Deucy. They called us things like that. And of course, we were expected to take the master's last name. Deucy Clayburn, that's what I had to answer to if

11

stopped by a white person wanting to know what I was doing, why I was doing it, and if I knew what was good for me I'd wipe that look off my face.

Guess I had something of my father in me that the Texan didn't cotton to.

My father always said his name was William, plain William. Wouldn't answer to any other. The only way Blade could get him to work—and they needed him for a thousand hard jobs that no one else could do—was to call him William. Mam told me how they'd *hear* the overseer grit his teeth as he forced himself to say, "All right, *William!* Get that there mule harnessed up and get out in the woods and start haulin'!"

A mulish fellow, my father. I am proud of him, proud of him . . .

Back to Cezanne Pinto.

Two things I've done well in my life. Understand horses, teach them gently. Understand children, teach them gently too.

Horses were first in my life. Teaching came after I'd scrambled my way into an education a long time later.

From the time I was a little fellow, I worked in the stables, usually sleeping in a box stall to keep a restless horse easy. I had the gift. Could gentle down, comfort, calm the most wayward, ornery piece of horseflesh on the plantation, and I grew up loving them more than anything in the world except Mam.

Clayburn had a stable master, name of Stebbins, a crude fellow, fond of the bottle, but not altogether a brute like Blade. Secretly (he hoped it was a secret, but *we* knew) Stebbins was afraid of horses. It made him a bad handler, apt to turn out head-shy, hard-mouthed, spooky mounts. I was just—goodness knows—maybe six or seven, when he came to me, all smiles and whiskey breath.

"Deucy," he said, rubbing my head roughly, "I cain't he'p noticin' that yore right handy aroun' the barn, you sho' got a way with horsh flesh. Blast their hides. So this yere is what Ah'm settlin' to do. Gonna larn you all Ah know. *Oversee* you. Unnerstan' what Ah'm sayin', eh, eh?" He leaned forward, squinting into my face, as if to make sure I comprehended spoken words.

"Yessuh, I unnerstan's," I said, adding, "Massa." You had to "Massa" all white men, but just one would do for such as Stebbins. With Clayburn or Blade it had to be repeated. A lot.

"Good, good," he went on, swaying a little. "Larn you every las' thing Ah know 'bout the stupid, ornery beasts—trainin' 'em up, ridin', teach 'em obedience, stan' to be mounted, behave their stupid selves an' so on an' forth. Watcha say to that, eh, eh, eh? Real ol' break for a nigger boy, eh, *eh?*"

"Yes*suh!*" said I, happy at the prospect before me.

It is interesting to note how the inward blaze of fury and hatred that the word, on a white person's tongue, causes me to feel now and has for so many years, wasn't a spark then. A term used so frequently, casually, even sometimes, I imagine, without intent to shame, I accepted as descriptive. A kitten was a cat, a colt a horse, a black person a nigger.

Long time changing . . . and so far to go.

Well.

That young, I began, in addition to exercising the horses—from the start there wasn't a one I couldn't ride—to break and train them under the "supervision" of Stebbins. We had horses for the plow and the carriages, we had saddle horses, hunters, ponies for children. I loved them all—the bright and biddable animals, and those that were nearly unteachable, having been early discouraged by Stebbins's handling.

Most of all, I loved that little filly Shenandoah, mine to bring up from the day she was born.

Of course, along with the other stable hands, I took care of tack, shined boots, groomed the animals, mucked out, kept the barouche, the two gigs, and the big carriage reasonably clean. And I was not spared a turn in the fields, usually just to take water out to the tobacco rows for the pickers to splash on their faces, drink from their hands.

One day I shall remember, always remember . . .

I'd gone out, lugging the bucket, trying not to splash, and came upon a field boss standing over an old man who was on his hands and knees between rows.

"What's the trouble, Uncle?" the boss was saying, without harshness, without concern. "Why ain't you workin' your share?"

The old man didn't stir, except to move his head

unhurriedly from side to side. "Man say whass de trubble, whass de trubble. Trubble enuff, sar, trubble enuff, nuttin' but trubble by day 'n' by night. I gwine dead dis night, git away from dis yere, go t' Jesus."

The field boss lifted his whip, let it fall to his side, and walked off shrugging. I sprinkled water on the old man's neck, cupped some in my hand and held it to his mouth, but he couldn't drink. He did die. That night, as he said he would.

"How did he know, Mam?" I asked, frightened. "How'd he know fer sure dat he dead dis night?"

Mam couldn't tell me.

Where the best horses were concerned, I took on jobs that Stebbins gradually relinquished as he "taught me all he knew."

I also helped Cupid, the blacksmith, till I became pretty good at shoeing a horse myself, provided it would stand still for a child. Cupid was not a bright man, but I was happy in his large, slow company, in his bright open forge. He had a harmonica that he kept hidden there. Taught me to play it. Old airs. Jubilee airs. Gospel airs. That most beautiful of American folk tunes, "Shenandoah." I learned to play them all on Cupid's little harmonica.

"Jes' don' do it roun' any a *dem*," he'd say, indicating everyone outside the forge, where he worked and lived. Only there did he feel safe, from owners, overseers, stable masters, even other slaves.

Clanging away in his fiery forge, Cupid used to sing a song he'd brought with him from Africa. He was a first-generation slave and would never speak of the trip over. His song, almost lost in the clang and clangor of the forge, went like this:

De ba-na co-ba, ge-ne me, ge-ne me, ge-ne me!
De ba-na co-ba, ge-ne me, ge-ne me, ge-ne me!
Ben d'nu-li, nu-li, nu-li, ben d'le . . .

He said it meant, in the tongue of his ancestors, "My soul need sumpin' dat's new, dat's new . . ."

"What new t'ing your soul need, Cupid?" I asked, only once.

He slapped his hands against his mouth, then said, "Doan wan' no new t'ing, no *way* atall. Jes' need de ol' way back. Wanna be back *dar*. Wish so *bad* Ah was back dar still. Gib my life up to be back on my own lan' fer a hour. Talk my own tongue fer a hour. Gib my life fer a hour—fer a *minute* of home . . ."

I never asked about the song again because the cureless longing in his voice made me hurt, and I didn't want to hurt.

Besides, those were good years for me. Because of Mam and Cupid. Because of the horses. In *spite* of everything else. After Mam was gone, and I moved through my days bone-bruised by loss, Cupid and the horses kept me sane.

Our ancestors communicated with drums. Over rivers and bush, across vast stretches of veldt, they told one another news of joy and mourning, birth and death, told gossip, sent warnings and greetings throbbing through miles of African air. When we came—when we were *brought*—to this country, to the slave world of the New World, the drums were taken from us, for fear of . . . us.

Oh, true, true . . . hedged round with power and terror were the planters, the slaveholders, of the South.

Fearful that we would speak among ourselves across the miles, on drums, in a language they couldn't understand. That we would scheme, plot uprisings. That within their very sight and hearing, under their very noses, we would build ourselves strong enough to topple them.

So the drums had to go.

So the grapevine had to come.

I recall the Big House lament: "Ah just cain't un-der*stand*! How do they *do* it? They learn what all's happened miles away before we heah a breath of it ourselves! Somethin' must be done! It must be stopped! It's right dangerous!"

It *was* dangerous.

We were dangerous.

They tried to hack down the knotty branches of the grapevine, rend its roots, wrench them from the earth. But it flourished.

We had a saying in the quarter: "Dere's a word you kin tell to de grapevine dat de grapevine doan tell back."

When I was very little, hearing that "de grape-vine" had told some secret thing to us in the quarter, I went to where the purple scuppernongs were climbing as though in a great cage, and sat listening for a long time before I went and asked Mam if the grapes only spoke to special people and who were they?

She laughed, and pulled me close, and explained that it was messages that flew from mouth to ear and that we called it the grapevine because the grapes were dark, and white ears couldn't hear dark voices.

Well.

The dark fruit of the grapevine whispered of slave revolts in Caribbean islands, where black people were masters now. The grapes spoke of an Underground Railroad running to states and territories in this country where slaves could throw their chains away and walk off free. All of us children, and plenty of grown-ups too uninformed to think otherwise, pictured the great snorting Freedom Train speeding through a tunnel deep in the ground, whistle screaming, smoke pouring from its stacks in glorious billowing clouds, till at length it roared up out of the earth to spill us, like the children of Israel, into the sunlight of the Promised Land.

From the first arrival of the first slave ship on these shores, thousands upon thousands of us ran toward liberty, not sure where to find it, knowing we could die without reaching it.

The plantation masters and their wives and children tried to overhear the tidings of the grapevine. They sent black spies among us . . . persons willing, for preference or pay, to prove false to any loyalty. But the grapevine never told, and master and mistress learned, too late, what it had been saying.

What it had foretold.

So.

The night before she was to go in the wagon to Texas, Mam and I stayed up late in our corner of the cabin in the quarter, eating a couple of biscuits she'd taken from their table. No candle, of course. We sat together in the dark, whispering.

"You call to min' ol' Magna?" Mam said.

"Course."

Magna was a lame field hand who one day escaped on a cow, rode away bareback in broad morning light. Magna was pretty old, likewise the cow. They didn't go after her.

I recall Clayburn and Blade sitting on a paddock fence, joking their fool heads off about it.

"Greatest darky escape in a coon's age!" Blade sputtered, tobacco juice dribbling down his chin. "Crippled crone forks spavined mount and *away they go!*"

Clayburn slapped his skinny thigh, laughing till I thought he'd fall off the fence. "Where all will they *get* to, do you reckon?"

"Wal, now . . ." Blade chewed, spat, grinned. "Mind, she's got a right good seat on a cow, has old Magna." This sent them into another gale of high spirits. "Might could make it—oh, what say to Georgia, eh?"

"Think so? Or could drown in the Dismal Swamp afore she got there."

"Wouldn't surprise me none. Old bones and new, anythin' it kin get, that there swamp'll take."

They sat in a while longer, chuckling at the good joke, then went off shaking their heads.

That they imagined an escaping slave would head south, I attribute to stupidity and an inability to think above the Mason-Dixon line.

Of course Magna did not ride her cow toward Georgia, or toward the Dismal Swamp. Of course she headed north, for a free state. I like to think she

22

reached a haven, had some fetterless peace for what years were left her. I want to believe that the cow made it too, and ended her days safely grazing.

Probably that's not what happened.

But *maybe*.

I like to believe a lot of things that might have been, so as not to dwell too much on things that were and are and no doubt will be.

So, there's Mam and me in the cabin, in the dark, whispering to each other, crying some, trying to say good-bye without believing that's what it was. But it was. I didn't know where in Texas they took her, and though years later, after the war, I went to Texas trying to find her, I never saw my mother again.

"When you gits a li'l older, son, you run fum dis place, hear?" she said, rocking me in her arms. "Get 'way fum dis place whar I won't be no more."

I must've been under eight at that time, because I was still wearing the tow-cloth singlet that slave children were given after they were two or three years old. Before that, we went naked, no matter the weather.

Tow-cloth? A coarse, itchy cotton made into a one-piece garment that came below our knees. After the age of eight, boys were given short pants, girls a long dress tied with string at the waist. We got new garments at the once-a-year issue day. Only grown-ups had shoes.

"Run whar to, Mam?" I asked timidly.

"Nort', lak your daddy. Pennsylvany, New Yawk, Canady. One a dem places whar freedom's at. Whar freedom, freedom, freedom's at."

"But *Mam*," I whispered, "Cupid say dey's a ribber a t'ousan' mile wide 'tween here 'n' de Nort'. He say nobody *nebber* made it to de Nort'. Thass slave talk, 'bout freedom, Cupid say. He say dey's no sich t'ing as black-skin freedom."

"Deucy! You knows pore Cupid's stupid."

"I likes him," I said stubbornly. "He larn me to play de *har*monica. Less me work de bellows. Cupid a *good* man. An' gentle wit' de hosses. Not like Stebbins."

"Nobody say stupid cain't be good. Jes' doan you lissen to de lies. Dat pore fool b'lieve what *anyone* tell him."

"He say he hear 'bout dat ribber right fum Blade hisself."

24

"You b'lieve what Blade tell we 'bout *anyt'ing?* How you t'ink your daddy made it t' New Yawk *City,* an' den back agin dat time he cum back, axin' we t' go 'long wit' him? T'ink your daddy could *swim* a t'ou-san' mile? T'ink he had a *boat* t' *sail* a t'ousan' mile? Doan you ebber, not ebber in your life, *lissen* t' Blade or any odder one a dem. Liars! Dey is *all* a *dem liars!* Say t'ings t' keep we skeert t' run. Well, your daddy warn't skeert, and doan you be, too, heah?"

"Den whyn't *we* run, you an' me? Run now, dis night. Get on up and hightail outa yere dis *minute.* Mam! Less you and me hightail to whar freedom's at." My voice was rising. "Dat way you cain't go t' Texas—"

"Hush!" she said. "Hush, my chile, my beloved, be*loved* chile."

I'll remember it—how she put her hand on my mouth, how her voice hoarsened as she spoke.

"Deucy, lissen. I'se too ol', too tired, an' t' tell de pity-fill trut', too skeert t' hightail it outa here, an' you is jes' too yong, see? I'd be skeert fer de two of we, los' in swampses and woodses. Hongry. Maybe cotched 'n' took back in chains 'n' sol' south—sol' down t' Natchez or New Orleens," she said, and shivered. Even to name those cities put fear in our voices.

She stopped and sighed as deep a sigh as ever I had heard, before she went on.

"Your daddy say dat up north jes' 'bout all a body see is white faces. I jes' could not stan' t' be in such a worl' a whiteness. Mought be I'd *like* t' be strong 'n' brave—like your daddy, like Magna, like Missus Tubman, but I ain't. Jes' ain't. Jes' ain't. Thass sumpin' you gotta understan', and *ax*cept. I'se a weak womans."

"No you ain't, Mam. *You* is a queen!"

I could feel her smiling in the dark. "Kitchen queen, Thass all." She rocked me back and forth. "One t'ing I always done, tol' you de trut', and I jes' done dat— tol' you a sad pity-fill trut'."

"Den I'se gwine run by mysel' t'morra," I said. "I doan wanna be yere when you'se . . . when you ain't . . . I'll 'scape t'morra, my ownsel'."

"No! No, no, no, no, *no!* You too yong t' mak' your way. You'se a baby still. Wait a bit, den you *run.* An' not on no cow. Take some hoss dat cottons t' you, lak dat little pinto filly yore so sot on. Wait till yore old 'nough t' run an' she's old 'nuff t' be rid, den go by night and doan stop till yore on free soil."

"Steal a *hoss*, Mam?" I said. Just a boy, understand, and used to obeying any white person that gave an order. It was sure one of them wasn't going to order me to swipe a horse and hightail it for freedom.

"Won't be stealing, no*how*," said Mam, hard-voiced. "You an' me an' your daddy and a t'ousan' t'ousan' folks now called away paid a t'ousan' t'ousan' time fer any hoss you mought ride offen on. She be *your own hoss*, a gif' fum we. You take her, when de time come."

For a while we were quiet, she holding me close, now and then kissing my head.

All at once she said, "You get shed of dis yere Deucy name, too, hear? Slave name. Bad as Cupid. When you go, tak unto you a good, homemade by your own-sel' name. Doan even take William, atter your daddy. A name for yoursel' alone, yoursel' alone."

"How I do dat, Mam?" I asked shakily.

Too much was being crowded on me there in the dark that night before I was to lose her forever. I was hungry, lonely in advance of being without Mam, terrified at being told I must run away on a horse belonging to Ol' Massa. "I doan know how to tak unto mysel' no name."

"We'll study on it right now, de two a we, see, see?"

Well, then.

What the Clayburns knew of the world beyond their pale, their own acres and desires, was meager. They'd have known the names of John Brown and Nat Turner, of Harriet Tubman and Sojourner Truth. These people were threats. But they'd not have heard mentioned Jean Baptiste Pointe Du Sable (*there's* a mighty name for you!) of Chicago.

Of Chicago? He *founded* the town.

There now—that's something you didn't know.

Jean Baptiste Pointe Du Sable was born on the island of Haiti, in the mid-eighteenth century. His mother was a slave, his father a rich white Frenchman who sent this boy of his to Paris to be *educated*. Think of it! Consider it carefully! There he was, half white, half black, by all odds fated to spend his life chopping in the canebrakes.

But!

He happened to have a white father who—think of it!—*loved him.*

It's kept me frowning and laughing all my years, to realize how luck plays dice with our lives.

Well, lucky Jean Baptiste—after countless adventures that Mam told of to keep me from crying in the night when I was hungry, or cold, or scared of Blade—landed in what later became the state of Illinois, where he founded a trading post and married a Potawatomi Indian woman. His business flourished, and his marriage was happy. He named his trading post Chicago, which means, in the Potawatomi tongue, "onion."

Chicago is an onion, and you didn't know that, either.

Years, and many lives, after life in the slave quarter, I took the Atchison, Topeka, and Santa Fe, bound for Chicago. Here I have lived, fallen in love, married. Here I have taught children, had children of my own. Here people I loved and could not spare left me anyway, to go down the long tunnel that leads to death.

Here in Chicago I have grown old.

To settle at last in the city that Jean Baptiste Pointe

29

Du Sable founded—I persist in believing that special legend—seemed natural. More important, the greatest friend, after Mam, that I ever knew had been teaching school there for some time.

At her stern urging, I scrambled my way into an education, then followed that proud straight back into the public school system of Chicago, where I remained, learning and teaching, for decades. I tried to share with my children the legacy life had given me. Some knowledge. Much affection. The lessons of pain. I tried to give them a sense of what we need to acknowledge—that the human species, in its many hues, with its many gods and countless ways of thinking and behaving, is braided together in one long, thick strand, and that if we don't come to understand—to concede—this large and simple truth, our world will ravel past repair.

Will we learn that? Learn in time to keep our poor little planet, and ourselves, from shredding apart? I hope so. That I shall be gone before the answer, one way or the other, is given us does not matter.

What matters is to learn in time.

*　　*　　*

So.

Back to Jean Baptiste Pointe Du Sable and his beautiful Indian wife, and how between them they altered my name and my life.

This lucky couple had a son and a daughter, and named one of them Cezanne. The grapevine's voice was blurry as to which.

Mam loved to tell of Jean Baptiste, tell the things she knew from the grapevine . . . about his birth, about his daddy who loved him and gave him a French education. About how he founded the city of Chicago. What she didn't know, she made up. Stories about his beautiful Indian wife, his great trading post, his educated children. When we huddled together after the long day's work, she'd tell me these tales.

Tales to keep the dark away, and fear away, and sorrow.

She'd describe Paris, which she knew nothing about. I've been there, and she wasn't far off at that. She said it was a beautiful city of church spires and bells, of balls and glittering lights and a dark, sparkling river. She said that in Paris a black person could feel free and warm and welcome. That's how it was when I was there, long ago.

It seems to me now that every place I ever saw, I saw long ago, that everything I ever did, I did long ago.

I feel as if my life took place long ago.

That last night, holding and hugging each other, Mam commanding me to run from the plantation when I was old enough, I with my heart cracked and crazed with pain because of what the morning would bring, we made up a name for me:

Cezanne Pinto.

We named me first for the son, or the daughter—we didn't care which—of Jean Baptiste Pointe Du Sable, and then for the pinto filly that was my special care at that time. She was nervous and frail and I was scared Ol' Massa would put her down if I didn't stand by her, give her confidence. She seemed to need me.

She'd escaped death by minutes. Clayburn didn't believe in giving a foal that seemed weakly a chance. If it wasn't on its feet and nursing within a half-hour of birth, it was put down as not worth rearing. When that little filly spilled out on the hay, she just stayed there, wet and trembling, the minutes moving her closer to death.

I was outside the stall, watching Mr. Clayburn. He was inside with his gun, ready to snuff this small life if it didn't pull itself together and prove worthy of oats and grooming and training and all that goes into raising a foal to useful adulthood.

I was shaking as much as she was, praying as hard as I could, *willing* her to stagger upward, even if she fell down right after.

"Jes' git on your feet," I whispered to her in my head. "Jes' mak a effort 'n' stan' up. Dey keep you den, ebben if you topples once't or twice't. Jes' *try* . . ."

She tried.

Head forward, she pushed her front legs up, splayed wide apart and nearly buckling, then sat awhile, rocking from side to side, her little tail sticking out behind like a feather duster. At last, when I was so frightened, thinking it beyond her strength, she shoved upward with her back legs and stood. Lurching this way and that, she took a step, keeled over, struggled up again, found her mother's teats and began to suck.

I was sniffling and gasping, trying not to make a sound, but Mr. Clayburn wheeled and saw me. He'd have slapped me down. Carelessly. An automatic clip on the jaw for any black face his eyes lit on. Then he saw who it was.

"Oh, it's you, Deucy," he said, yawning. "Take over. If anyone can keep her goin', it'll be you. Durned if I know why they should take to a black imp more'n they do to me or my stable master, but facts is facts. Mind, I want her to get on proper or I'll take it outa your woolly head."

"Yes, Massa," said I.

If you didn't Massa him every other sentence, he'd know the reason why, and the reason could involve anything from that absentminded clip across the side of your face to a beating by Blade with people invited to look on, watch the entertainment. They got so bored at the Big House that even slave floggings, which they must've seen hundreds of times, served to pass the time.

("Mama, which would y'all rather do today—ride over an' listen to Mary Belle Makins practice tryin' to play on her piana, or jus' stroll down to the quarter 'n' watch a whippin'?"

"Ah declare—it's too hot for either, less jus' set on the po'ch 'n' have some *lemonade*.")

"I sho' watch her good, Massa," I told Clayburn eagerly.

"You better."

"She got a name, Massa? You name her yet?"

"Yep. Miss Mady says if it's a filly, she's Shenandoah."

"Thass a *nice* name, Massa."

I wanted to say it was a beautiful, a glorious name, but I held my tongue. He scowled at my having an opinion at all, but went off without hitting me.

Miss Mady was Clayburn's eldest daughter, the only one who cared about the horses. No one else in that family could have thought up such a lovely name for a foal.

From that day, Shenandoah, named for a river, and I, named by my mother and me for a great black man's child and a pretty little horse, were like brother and sister.

Horses are as different from one another as we are— some intelligent and curious and affectionate and willing to learn. Others lazy and incurious and unintelligent, almost unreachable. There are unnumbered variations between.

But *every* horse is born prepared to be terrified.

They fear strange places, people, sights, sounds. A blowing leaf, an oddly shaped stone, the unexpected appearance of a rabbit in the path, will cause a leap skyward, followed by flight—from the menace of a rabbit, a leaf, a stone in the road. They are frightened of their own shadows. Many a horse, trotting peacefully, shadow unseen behind him, will, if it swings suddenly in front, bolt and take to his heels, sometimes throwing an unprepared rider.

It is my opinion that all the so-called "lower" animals are born frightened—and they have reason. It is very very dangerous for them, sharing a planet with us "higher" animals.

Stebbins, I think I've said, didn't succeed in spoiling all the creatures under his whip, especially after he devised his scheme of "overseeing" my work, but by then he had made far too many irreclaimable animals out of colts that came into the world willing to do their best.

*   *   *

For my part—and only because the horses trusted me—I was more fortunate than any but the servants in the Big House. Of the stable boys, I alone was allowed to train fillies for the ladies of the plantation to ride. Ol' Missus, and the Clayburn daughters, that was. They were an indolent lot, and only one, Miss Mady, rode regularly. She was the only white person who sometimes looked at me as if she and I belonged to the same species. Not to the same race, and way below her *level*. But she did not always seem to find me indistinguishable from plantation livestock.

She rode as prettily as any young lady in the county. Nice balance in the saddle, easy hands on the reins, gentle conveyer of signals to her mount. She never went out alone, for fear of accidents, and as the other two weren't happy on anything peppier than a rocking chair, it often fell to me to accompany Miss Mady on her daily excursions around the broad acres of Gloriana. She had a fine silver-studded English saddle. Except when breaking fillies and mares to the saddle, I rode bareback in those years.

Frequently Miss Mady took us far afield, to neighboring houses where she would go in for tea and talk, leaving me and the horses to stand waiting, no matter what the weather. Many a time I got drenched, shivered from cold, was scared witless by lightning and thunder, got tired to dropping, waiting for her to come out again.

But then, on the way back, she'd sometimes address a remark to me.

"Look, Deucy! The kingfisher there on the bank? Is he not beautiful?"

"Yes ma'am, Miss Mady. He sho' is."

Having recognized my presence, she was apt to ride along, humming to herself for a while. Then: "Come on, Deucy! I'll race you!"

Off we'd go, thundering over a grassy lea, the wind rushing past in clovery fragrance, and for a space I'd be absolutely happy. It's possible that only when riding was *she* entirely happy.

"There now, Deucy," she'd say, as we slowed to a lope, a trot, a walk—she, of course, having won the race. "Wasn't that *fun?*"

"Sho' was, Miss Mady."

Back at the stables, I'd help her to dismount, then walk the horses as she went toward the Big House, confident, I am confident, of having made the pickaninny happy as all get-out, actin' like he was quite the little human bein'.

("Mady, you take care now, and don't go spoilin' that darky, givin' him *ideas!*"

"Don't fret yoursel', Mama. I know better'n to go too far with him. Cain't have *any* of them forgettin' their *place.*")

Nevertheless, in looking back, I concede that my lot was far far better than most children knew on a plantation. At the Big House because Miss Mady wanted me in good shape to ride. In the quarter, no doubt, because the slaves, house and field, admired my father for having beaten up the breaker. Mam not only was the wife of this heroic man, but had a radiance innate to herself.

My mother may have been afraid to run away, first with my father, and years later with me, into the woods and swamps, searching for freedom but perhaps bringing us death, or—far worse—capture and the chain gang headed for Natchez or New Orleans. She was also, I have said and won't mind saying again, a queenly woman. Beautiful of face, willowy of form, low of voice. And so kind. Such a gentle, such a lovely woman was my mam.

My mother.

She was also a very good cook, adept at smuggling food out of the kitchen into the quarter to share it with the rest of us there.

I was the beneficiary of my father's courage and my mother's gentle, generous nature.

And then—I had some mettle of my own. A way with horses, of course, but also some interior cussedness that made me, even as a rather timid child, aware that no one was going to keep me in leading strings forever. There was, there is, something of that man who beat the breaker, something of William, in me.

It was dark—the moon, white as a camellia, still hung in the sky, a mist lay over the yard—on the morning the Texan's wagon, drawn by a span of eight sad-eyed oxen, pulled up early to the quarter. Mam and I waited outside the cabin, shivering, wordless. The wagon was already occupied by several silent black men and women, of the age and appearance to be called "prime field hands," who'd doubtless been bought at neighboring estates.

"Up now," the Texan said to my mother, not too roughly. "Got a long pull ahead of us."

Mam drew me against her, whispered in my ear, "My heart pinned to your heart, Cezanne. Fo'ebber 'n' ebber . . . my heart pinned to yourn, to yourn, to yourn . . ."

Clayburn, who'd come to see the Texan off, looked from her to me, pulled at his beard, and grunted. "I got a gel, Mady, says they maybe keer 'bout each other same as white folks. Don't put credit in the notion myself, seein' as how the good Lord made us different as night and day—"

He snorted at his own witticism.

The Texan stared at him coolly, shrugged, hoisted himself to the driver's seat without replying.

My mother sat with her back straight, her eyes meeting mine, as the wagon moved slowly out of the muddy yard and down the rutted road. Gazing at her white headcloth, her upraised arm, I waved until the wagon went around a bend and was gone.

Afterwards, people in the quarter were kind to me. We were nearly all good to one another in our bondage, in our wretchedness. But there was no one I could *count* on. Slaves were auctioned away, ran away, took sick, died. I was on my own, waiting for the years to pass until I'd be old enough, and Shenandoah old enough, so we could run away.

Long years they were, long time passing.

If sometime in the future, someone should read this history—though it is possible that I write for myself alone—the question must arise: How did he learn his letters?

This is how it came about, and how I came to be a teacher, after a few years herding cattle up the Chisholm Trail:

Here and there, now and then, the mistress of a plantation (never, oh never, the master) would undertake to teach a favored house slave to read. Then it was but a step to writing. And then? Ah—like the couple in the Garden long ago, once we bit of the apple, once we *tasted* the forbidden fruit that grew on the Tree of Knowledge, once we knew the savor of a little learning, nothing was ever the same again.

Not for us, the servants. Not for them, the masters.

They were noble, those Southern women who vi-

olated, at terrible risk to themselves, the rigid Southern tradition of keeping us slaves in the Swamp of
Ignorance. But kings and tyrants, emperors and dic-
tators, have always known that to keep a people in
harness, you put blinders on them, sealing away the
light of learning.

Learning!
To know how to read! To know how to write!
What might it not lead to?
What *did* it not lead to?

Frederick Douglass was taught the rudiments of
reading by his mistress, Mrs. Auld of Baltimore. Until her husband discovered what was going on and
put a stop to it. "You will forever unfit him to be a
slave!" he bellowed. "You will undermine our way of
life! These darkies are content with their lot. Leave
it at that! Let them start thinking for themselves, it
could lead to disaster, to the downfall of all we hold
dear!"

Mrs. Auld quickly stopped the boy's lessons. Too
late, too late! She had put his foot on a path from
which he would not turn back. She had unfitted him,

indeed, to be a slave. The arduous years of learning, he related in his book, with a better pen than mine by far.

Read it! Read it! Read that book!

I learned my letters in a kitchen school.

Tamar, who replaced Mam in the kitchen, was in every way different from her, except that they were both fine cooks. Mam was a quiet person who tried not to be noticed, and though she'd have fought bears to protect me, slavery had otherwise given her the air of a creature at bay.

We children regarded the new cook, who had a voice like a bullfrog's and was so tall we had to bend our heads back to meet her eyes, with astonishment.

"Aunty higher'n a piney tree," we said to one another in awe. "Ain't hardly no *mans* kin reach her."

All black grown-ups were addressed by us as "Aunty" or "Uncle." (Properly, we should have called Cupid "Uncle," but it confused him, so he remained "Cupid" to all.)

Tamar didn't so much arrive among us as detonate. She wore her colored turbans starched and twisted high into cone shapes, so that she towered over everyone except the biggest of field hands. The master himself seemed to shrink in her presence. She was muscular as a man, and seemed afraid of nothing and no one.

She did interesting things to the Clayburns' food before sending it to the dining room. As the glories of Gloriana were never found in the vast kitchen that lay at the back of the house, and Mr. Clayburn perhaps didn't even know where it was located, they were ignorant of her practices. I don't think she actually made any of them sick.

There was little family feeling among the Clayburns. Ol' Missus usually kept to her rooms, fanning herself and "feelin' po'ly." Once a week the cook and the butler would go to her sitting room and consult about the week's menus and plans. Mam had told me how these brief interviews went. Mrs. Clayburn uniformly held a cologned handkerchief to her nose with one hand, waved the other about, and said, "Y'all decide. Ah'm feelin' po'ly."

Her daughters stopped in to see her occasionally, but occupied most of their time either visiting nearby plantations or entertaining at home . . . teas, dinners, balls, picnics. They did a lot of eating and dancing, a deal of talking and no reading. The only book in the house was a large Bible bound in white leather, and Mam said she never saw anyone reading in it. With a stable of wonderful mounts, only Miss Mady cared to ride.

In truth, they were an insipid and idle family, and I wonder they didn't go mad with boredom.

Back to the kitchen school.

Sundays, on the plantations, field hands did not labor. Many went to church, always with at least one white man in the congregation, there to make sure no one went beyond *praying* for happiness, to be arrived at in the next world, not sooner. Others got drunk, if they could lay hold of some corn likker. Many slept the entire day and night, since their hours of sleep on weeknights were limited to three or four. A few house servants were obliged to work, as the family had to be served. But in general, it was a relaxed day for us slaves, with even floggings put off till Monday.

The Clayburns, like much of the "Quality" (which

46

they considered themselves to be but were not), spent Sunday mornings at church, afternoons paying or receiving calls. Even Ol' Missus bestirred herself for the Sabbath. Interested in no souls but their own, they didn't bother about ours. This left us children, and those grown-ups who hoped it would prove helpful when they ran away, to attend the new cook's kitchen school.

Tamar had learned to read and write when she'd been nursemaid to the children of a widow woman in Maryland.

"She was one strange pale person," the new cook told us. "Couldn't seem to tell black from white, *or* care. We was all the same to her, almos' like she couldn't *see*. Taught me to read from de Bible 'n' make my letters as good as she could her ownself."

"How come you to leave dis strange white widda womans, Aunty?" we'd ask, and Tamar would lift her heavy shoulders.

"She married again, 'n' dat man like to *explode* when he foun' I could read better'n hisself. Ignorant fool of a jackass. Handsome as sin, thass how he cotched her, pore soul. She look at that face 'n' doan look fer a minute to see what all's lurkin' behin' it. I expec' her life is a mis'ry to this day. He sol' me at auction," she'd conclude. "Man afore dis yere Clayburn. Dat one sol' me too."

"*Why*, Aunty?" we'd ask, never tiring of the answer. "Why dey sol' off a gran' ol' cook like y'all?"

"I plain was too *tall* fer 'em. Shrimpy mens, both a dem. Hadda stan' on dere tippy-toes 'fore dey reach to my chin. So—I am yere wit' y'all, 'n' Ol' Massa tall hisself, so mebbe I stays. Now, git your books out."

Our "books" were scraps of paper on which she had written the alphabet, which we had first to memorize, and then write out with bits of chalk and crayon. When we had those down to her satisfaction, she commenced to read to us from a schoolbook of children's Bible stories, taken, with her mistress's blessing, from that long-ago nursery. (She had a copy of the King James Bible as well, carefully wrapped in oilcloth, treasured above anything else she owned.) After each paragraph, she would patiently show us how to copy it on our pieces of paper. Gradually, over months, years, of furtive instruction, those of us who were persistent enough, obstinate enough, learned how to read, how to write.

Tamar knew the Bible—I really think by heart—and spoke a finer English than the Clayburns could. She was careful not to do so, even when they were out of hearing. Informers were among us, and a fine-talking slave might be told on, and so deemed "uppity." *No* good, no good *ever* came from being known as an "uppity darky." Only, and much, trouble came of it, and Tamar did not look for trouble. She seemed content to teach those who wanted to learn, otherwise to stay in the kitchen, away from the rest of the household, sending meal after meal to the family table—watching with her rogue's smile as Herkimer bore the fancy covered dishes away.

Oh, yes—Tamar unfitted a lot of children and a few grown-ups to be slaves.

As months passed, she and I grew fond, grew close. In part because I was her most eager pupil. In part through shared loss and sorrow. She had had all her children sold away from her, I my only mother. We looked for comfort in each other and, in some measure, found it.

Tamar. Mrs. Auld, before she was found out. The pale Maryland widow woman who couldn't tell black from white. Gone now, gone long since. They have, always have had, my blessings.

Shenandoah grew up to be the sweetest little pinto filly that ever went through her paces.

"Purty as a spotted pup under a red wagon," Stebbins said, again and again, shaking his head as if he couldn't believe what he saw. Knowing her, being around her, had, astonishingly, made him somewhat gentler with other animals. A teacher—in her own way—was the beauteous Shenandoah.

"Oh, you precious li'l *darlin'!*" Miss Mady would say, throwing her arms around Shenandoah's neck, laying her cheek against the filly's face. "You angel horsy, you should have *wings!*"

Cupid, just before her first shoeing, took Shenandoah's head between his huge hands and placed a kiss upon her forehead, where there was a white blaze like a star.

"Nuttin' on two laigs or four ebber as purty as y'all, Shandy gal," he'd tell her.

The name Shenandoah had more syllables than Cupid cared to be bothered with. To him, she was Shandy.

Many years later, in Chicago, I encountered a sentence in a biography of Mathew Brady, the great Civil War photographer. (He, by the way, was a black fellow. Anyway half of him was. He had an Irish father and a black mother. Another interesting fact for you to put in your book, if you're keeping one.) Asked what had impelled him to go to the front and put the face of war on film, he replied: "A spirit in my feet said 'Go!' and I went."

One Sunday in May, when Shenandoah was nearly three years old, the kin of that spirit entered my boy's feet, and I decided that the time of deliverance was come, that we were old enough, she and I, to run from the plantation and find ourselves a new life in the North.

Early in the morning, after the other horses had been turned out to graze, I went to her stall, to explain my plan. She greeted me—she always did—by nibbling at my face with her soft lips, with little nickers of welcome that were a cordial to my heart.

"Shenandoah," I whispered, looking from one long-lashed brown eye to the other, "we's gonna run, you 'n' me. Fin' our freedom away fum dis yere place. Y'all reckon thass a good plan fer us two?"

She tossed her head, nickered again, then looked impatiently toward the broad meadow where fillies and colts, and mares with their foals, were racing about in the thick sweet grass, kicking up their heels, scratching one another's withers, play-fighting, bucking for the joy of the morning and their unbridled, uncurbed liberty. Horses are not hermits. Without the companionship of other horses, they grow dispirited.

I knew then that Shenandoah would not be going with me. Perhaps I'd known it all along. I would be running toward freedom and a life worth living. If I made it.

But this little horse was already free in a joyful world. Here on the plantation she was safe, well fed, cherished. She passed her days in the company of horses she knew, with human beings who loved and protected her.

I offered a dangerous journey to an unknown world, hard traveling, probably hunger, maybe a hard death.

I couldn't do that. Standing with my head against hers, patting her sturdy rump, I knew I was saying good-bye to Shenandoah.

Just then Cupid crossed the yard, glanced into the stable, walked in and said, "What y'all doin', Deucy, weepin' tears on dat dere hoss? She *sick?* Lemme look—"

"She ain't sick, Cupid," I said, blinking, rubbing my eyes with hard knuckles. "She jes' fine." I looked at him for a long moment, then said, "Cupid, I'se gwine t' run."

His mouth opened, but no words came.

"Doan tell nobody," I said, but knew he would not. "I figger I'm ol' 'nuff now to hightail it outa here, go fin' my mammy. Fin' my *mother*."

"Y'all know where all she at?" he croaked.

"Texas."

"Deucy. *Chile*. Texas is t'ousan's 'n' t'ousan's a miles from dis yere. An' big. I heared tell how Texas bigger'n all the rest of—" He windmilled his arms. "You nebber gonna fin' your mammy. In no *manner* will you do dat. Better not run, Deucy. You mought could drown, or get cotched by the patty-roller and beaten daid. Or be tooken back yere. What kin'a life you have iffen dey cotched you and brang you back? You mought be sold down de *ribber*."

"What kin'a life I have now?"

"Better'n lotsa folks roun' yere," he said grumpily.

It was true. It was not enough. I thought then, I think now, that the meanest existence as a free person is better, by so far that there is no measurement for it, than the easiest life as a slave, a prisoner.

Thousands of us thought the same. Some ran from lives so wretched that the risk of death was preferable, but there were those living more than comfortably—like James Christian, servant to President Tyler in the White House, having it real easy there—who fled away.

Freedom!

What we all dreamed on, and many died to reach.

Knowing he'd keep silence, I said, "I had a idea I mought tak Shenandoah 'long wit' me when I runs—"

Cupid looked bewildered, then angry, then downright sorry for me.

"Lemme ax you sumpin', Deucy," he said. "Lemme jes' ax you dis yere. How far you s'pose a black-blood boy like y'all gwine get on a blue-blood hoss like dat dere Shandy? You is plain *stoopid*—sich a jackass fool notion."

I sighed and nodded. "I knows dat, Cupid. I was t'inkin', not doin'. But I gwine miss her sumpin' horrible."

The blacksmith patted my head with his big hand. "Tell you, Deucy. You cain't tak dat dere hoss, no way, but I got sumpin' you kin tak on your runaway. Sumpin' to 'member ol' Cupid by."

"I warn't plannin' to fergit you, Cupid."

"I knows dat. Jes' de same . . ." He walked across the yard to his forge, returned in a moment, looking around to be sure he was unobserved. "Tak dis yere," he said, thrusting the harmonica at me. "Keep you comp'ny when yore alone or skeert or troubled wit' 'flictions."

I didn't make even a conventional protest. It was such a glorious gift that I could only throw my arms around him and murmur against his great chest, "T'ank you t'ank you, Cupid. You is—is wunnerful to me. You is bin my fren'." I turned the little thing around in my hand, put it to my mouth, and blew a few bars of "Shenandoah."

O Shenandoah, I long to hear you. Way, hey, you rollin' river!

"Thass jes' sweet as honeycake," Cupid said gently.

O Shenandoah, I'm bound to leave you . . .

"Course you'se boun' to leave 'er," he said, his voice filled with pity. "No way outa dat, Deucy."

I let Shenandoah, the beautiful little filly who had been like my sister since the day she was born, out of her stall and watched as she raced to the meadow, whickering, skipping, tossing her hind legs, flicking her pert tail, happy to join her friends.

"G'bye, g'bye," I called after her wordlessly. "My heart pinned to your heart, Shenandoah, pinned to your heart, to your heart . . . G'bye, sweet Shenandoah . . ."

"Blade comin'," Cupid warned. He stomped back to his forge, giving the overseer a sour glance.

When Blade had gone behind the barn, I walked slowly up to the Big House, around back to the kitchen, where Tamar was alone, baking biscuits.

"Mouf down roun' your shoeses, Deucy," she said. "Whass de matter? Biscuit wit' jelly benefit your spirits some?"

Unable to answer, I sat at the table, dropped my head on my arms, and cried. Luck and the hour of the Sabbath day kept us alone during my storm of grief and fear. Tamar waited until I'd choked myself out of tears, then put her hand heavily on my shoulder. I found the pressure comforting.

"Now, tell me," she said, sounding a different person from what I'd known till then. "What's troubling you so?"

Hands to my face, I rocked back and forth, gulping and sniffling.

Tamar buttered a couple of biscuits, slathered them with her quince jelly, poured a glass of milk, and said, "Imbibe! Then we'll talk."

It tasted so good, and as usual I was so hungry that in spite of my terror and despair, I ate and drank.

Then we did talk, quickly, quietly, for fear of lurking spies—those servants who stayed on the right side of Clayburn by betraying other servants, some of them friends.

When she understood that I was going to run, that nothing now would stop me, Tamar said, "Very well, then. We'll go together."

Sometimes you encounter the words, "My heart stopped with surprise." That's impossible, and yet it felt to me, that morning in the kitchen of Gloriana, when Tamar made that calm announcement, as if my heart suspended action, dangled inside me, too stunned to beat.

I said, "You means dat, Aunty? True 'nuff, you gonna run wit' me?"

"I never say what I don't mean," she answered in her deep, plum-colored voice. "Now, Deucy, we have to plan. What to take, when to go . . ."

"You talkin' dif'rent fum how you use-ta talk, Aunty."

"Yes. You will too, after a while. After we've been together for a time. I taught you to read, now I'll teach you to speak."

"Dat's good," I said.

She started to correct me, then spoke instead of getting together truck for the trip. Victuals—some salt herring, a few corn cakes—a knife, a net for fishing, matches, a couple of blankets. Not too much to carry, but enough to give us a degree of comfort.

"When we'se gwine go?" I asked, turning all decisions over to her.

"Now."

"*Now?*" I said, my legs going weak.

"If we're going, we'd best go right away. Wait, and word's sure to get out somehow—then you and I'd be shuffling to Natchez in neck irons by nightfall. Have you told anyone except me about this?"

"Cupid," I whispered. "I tol' Cupid. He nebber tell on we."

"Of course not. But notions get about, Deucy. Notions are like garter snakes wriggling through the grass, parting it in a path that anyone can see."

"Dey cute li'l fellas."

"But carry messages."

"Dey *do?* Lak de grapevine?"

She smiled. "Just teasing."

"Oh. Dat's a'right, den. But I ain't Deucy no mo," I said, lifting my head, meeting her eyes. "My name Cezanne. Cezanne Pinto."

"That's a *fine* name. Cezanne. Cezanne Pinto. I like that just fine."

"Mam and me, we did it up togedder, de night afore she—she got tooken off to Texas."

Tamar nodded, but offered no sympathy, rightly judging that it might start another freshet of tears.

Instead, she unwound the high bright starched turban from her head and replaced it with a faded bandanna, then went into the cook's room off the kitchen and came back carrying a couple of cotton blankets into which she wrapped the other truck she'd mentioned, along with her oilcloth-wrapped King James Bible.

She was so efficient that I couldn't help saying, "You ack lak yore a'ready to run, lak you got ever'-thin' sot in your haid."

"I was waiting for a sign. Now you have given it me." She looked about the kitchen, her mouth pursed in thought. "Guess that's it. Now, see here, Deu— Cezanne. You will have to do exactly as I tell you, understand?"

"Oh, yes'm. I'se in your han's. An' skeert. Dere's patty-rollers all about, 'n' what iffen dey see we 'n' ax what we'all doin' walkin' along by our ownsel's—"

"That's what I mean when I tell you to do what I say. *They*"—she used the word contemptuously, so I knew of whom she spoke—"are at church and then they'll be making calls, leaving cards, jabbering, slopping juleps. Even patty-rollers aren't apt to work on Sunday. Getting drunk in some tavern, more likely.

60

But if anybody—anybody at all—questions us, there's not to be a word from you. Is that clear?"

"Yes'm, Aunty."

"Now, Cezanne. We have two important documents."

"We does?"

"This," she said, spreading on the table a wrinkled, brownish old piece of paper, "is a map. I copied it, years ago, from the floor of a slave cabin in Maryland. Harriet Tubman *herself* drew it there in the dirt, so that runaways would know how to make it to the North, if she couldn't be with them. So they'd know which places were safe to stop on the Underground Railroad route."

"We sho' 'nuff gwine ride on dat dere *train*, Aunty?" I said, breathless with excitement. "How dat train get unnerneat' de groun'? How it do dat, atall?"

"Child. Cezanne. Listen to me . . . it's *called* the Underground Railroad and I don't know who named it, but what it is is—" She closed her eyes, exhaled, and said, "There's no time now. I'll explain on the way. *This*," she said, indicating the other paper, "is our pass."

"*Pass?*"

"Pass. To show, if anyone asks. Written by Mr. Clayburn, saying we two are free to go to the river to wash our clothes." She pointed to the bundle. "That is our washing."

I stared, bewildered. "How you get Massa to sign dat dere pass fer us?"

For a moment she looked impatient, then drew me against her briefly, in a manner so affectionate that I wanted to melt into her.

"Deucy, try to think clearly! Sorry—I mean *Cezanne*. I wrote the pass myself a few minutes ago. Chances are we won't be stopped, and if we are, chances are the patty-rollers or whoever questions us won't be able to read and chances are that if they can read they'll just believe what it says. Why shouldn't they? Everybody around here knows Clayburn, and everybody knows we only get to do our own chores, our washing and mending and so forth, of a Sunday."

"Dat's a gen'rous lotta *chances are*, Aunty."

"And we are obliged to take them *all*. Now, Cezanne—let us go forward!"

We marched out the kitchen door, she with the

bundle of "laundry" on her head, I with Cupid's harmonica in my shirt pocket.

It was sunhigh as we started on our way to freedom.

Freedom!!!!!!

CHAPTER TWO

Balancing the blanket bundle on her head, Tamar, in a pair of men's boots, tried to adjust her stride to mine as we walked down a rutted, pebbly dirt road. Even so, I had to run a little to keep up, and feet less toughened than those of a slave child might have found the road a sore trial, but my soles were impervious as leather. I have fine straight toes to this day, for having gone so many years unshod.

To either side of us were pastures where workhorses, mules, and cattle grazed, they not being entitled to crop the rich meadow grass that Shenandoah and her friends had sole possession of.

As we went along Tamar identified roadside weeds aloud. It was to keep me from thinking, I am sure, and oh, how well I recall her husky voice saying, "I shall give you the appellations of these humble plants, Cezanne, and you will repeat their names after me.

65

In this manner, we shall pass the time, and you will learn something perhaps not of great importance, but interesting nonetheless."

"*Apple-ashuns*, Aunty?" I said, puzzled.

"Nomenclature. I am giving you the *nomenclature*, which is another word for 'appellations'—the plain word is 'names'—of these flowers known to most of us as weeds. Never," she added, "use a simple word if you have at hand a fancy one."

(Tamar used to make statements like that. My favorite was: "Let no one persuade you that there are two sides to every question. There is only one side to *any* question.")

They have beautiful appellations, these hardy independent plants that grow wild, often rampant, in woods and fields, marshes and roadsides.

Thornapple, steeplebush, hawkweed, Queen Anne's lace—that's wild carrot—corn lilies, field pussy-toes. There was a ragged little sunflower called elecampane. I liked that. "*Elecampane*," I said to myself, over and over, and indeed it kept me, briefly, from realizing how afraid I was of what we were up to, what we were going toward.

To this day I can say without stumbling, "Thornapple, steeplebush, hawkweed, Queen Anne's lace—that's wild carrot—corn lilies, field pussy-toes, and *elecampane*." It's an incantation, a spell to summon up the image of Tamar, tall and terrible in her determination, keeping fear at bay as she named roadside flowers that people called weeds.

Oh, she was a bold brave Amazon of a black slave woman! I understand that Harriet Tubman was a small person, and Tamar, like Sojourner Truth, was bigger than most men, but inside each was an identical spirit that said to the enemy, "I will do what I am meant to do, what I have sworn to do! *Stop me if you can!*"

Sojourner Truth, luminous illiterate, swayed thousands with her drumroll preachment invoking freedom for black people, for women of all colors.

Mrs. Tubman led three hundred black men, women, and children through the Underground Railroad to freedom and, as she said, "never lost a passenger."

Now Tamar was making her first strike for freedom, leading her first runaway out of slavery.

She didn't lose me.

*   *   *

We'd gone a mile and some, when a horse and rider came slowly toward us. A white man, spitting a stream of tobacco juice, slouched in the saddle as if sick.

Tamar didn't break her stride. I was so frightened I thought I'd fall to the ground, or get sick myself. The nomenclature of wildflowers was of no help. "Aunty!" I whimpered. "What we gwine *do* iffen he stop we?"

"You are going to keep your mouth shut," she snapped. Then, as the rider drew near and reined in, she bobbed a curtsy, the "laundry" secure as if nailed to her head.

"Where y'all think yore goin', Mammy?" the man asked, sounding tired and uninterested.

"Jes' down to dat dere crick, Massa," Tamar said, waving in the direction of the orchard, beyond which ran a sizable creek. "We'se gwine warsh ar closes up. Marse Clayburn say we kin do dat."

"Clayburn? You his culluds?"

"Yessuh, Massa. Dat's us, right 'nuff."

"How do I know he says you kin do what you say he says you kin?"

Tamar took the pass from her pocket and held it

toward him. "Doan dis yere paper tell lak I say? Marse tol' me it say let dese two darkies go down to crick 'n' wash dey closes."

For a moment it looked as if he'd lean over and examine the paper; then he gulped, closed his eyes, swayed in the saddle, lifted the reins, and went on.

Tamar looked after him scornfully. "Fool jackass so drunk, or sick from getting over being drunk, he probably couldn't *see* the writing, much less read it."

We continued down the road.

Presently she turned away from it and led us through the orchard down to the creek. It was actually a little brook that bounded along, sliding glassily over stones, swirling around fallen sticks, warbling as it went its way.

"Now," she said. "We shall walk up this diamond rivulet a good long distance. That way, the hounds won't pick up our scent."

"You t'ink dey gwine set de *dawgs* on we, Aunty?"

"I do." She studied my face for a moment. "You can still turn back. You know I wouldn't blame you *at all*. It's a terrible thing to be frightened, and you are terribly frightened."

My throat felt constricted, my arms and legs limp, and I was finding it suffocatingly difficult to breathe.

"Let's set a spell," she said, lowering her bundle to the creek bank. "We're safe here for a short while, but they'll soon discover that no one's in the kitchen cooking. So. I repeat—you can run back now and no one will be the wiser. That fool on horseback won't remember us, and you can say, if they ask, that you never saw me. But you must make up your mind now, child."

"You sho' 'nuff gwine go on, your ownsel'?"

"Of course. I'd not start such a—such an *adventure* and not see it through any way I can. I won't say for certain that I'll reach freedom, but I won't turn my face from it now. I am on my way!"

"It's a *a'venture* we'se doin'?"

"For sure it's one I am doing. I welcome you to come with me, and I understand if you can't. But decide now, Deucy. I can't wait."

I've always believed she called me Deucy deliberately. To remind me that Deucy was a slave, whereas Cezanne would be a boy headed for freedom . . . if he could make it.

"I'se *comin'* wit' you!" I declared.

"Good. Up then." She took her boots off, handed them to me. "Carry these, please." Putting the bundle on her head, she steadied it and stepped into the stream.

I splashed in after her, enjoying the rush of cool water swirling about my legs, all at once abrim with the exhilaration of being on an adventure *for sure.*

We marched north for a couple of hours, sharing the creek with frogs and fish. Turtles toppled off logs at our approach. A breeze ruffling the willows, the songs of mockingbirds and meadowlarks, the purling water, kept us from speaking.

Just as I thought I could go no further, Tamar stepped up on the bank, and sat with a thump. After a few minutes, she undid the blanket bundle, took one salt herring and one corn cake from it, cut them in two with her knife.

"Let's have us a picnic, Cezanne!"

"Picnic? Lak de white folks hab?"

"Exactly. Now—I see a bush yonder crammed to bursting with blackberries. We'll dine on fillet of herring and corn bread, then move over there and have ourselves a berryful feast."

We picnicked in the clover, beside the fluent brook. Grasshoppers sprang about us greenly, birds leaned out of the willows to see us. God, said Tamar, was watching too, approving of our adventure.

"Sho' 'nuff?" said I. "He wan' we to run away?"

"He does. He thinks it's the exact right thing for us to do. God never said a body can only be free that's white and owns a big house and cane or tobacco fields, or cotton. *Or* slaves."

"Blade say He do. Blade say God an' de debbil do a pack togedder. White's free, black ain't."

"What would a scoundrel like Blade know of *God's* mind?" She lifted her gaze, and with an air of contentment. "But I'll warrant Satan's getting a real nasty surprise ready for that white devil, when the time comes."

"Dat's *good*," I said, elated at the thought of Blade's coming face-to-face with Satan himself.

We drank from the clear creek waters when we'd finished eating. Then, squashing the flowers and stems of a pretty little pink called Bouncing Bet, we lathered our feet, faces, hands, and washed up.

"We can rest a moment yet," Tamar said, aware

72

that though I could ride all day, I was not used to walking.

Drawing the harmonica from my pocket, I asked, "A'right iffen I blows on dis a bit, Aunty?"

"Oh, yes. But softly, Cezanne. Softly."

So, softly, I played my favorite air.

O Shenandoah, I long to hear you. Way, hey, you rollin' river! O Shenandoah, I long to hear you. Way, hey, we're bound away, 'Cross the wide—Missouri.

To me Shenandoah was my little pinto filly, no matter how many rivers shared her name, but I supposed the wide Missouri was a river too.

"That's so lovely. You play so sweetly, so sweetly," Tamar said.

"Cupid done larn me." I saw her hesitation, and asked, "Sumpin' wrong 'bout dat?"

"Oh dear. What can I say? Cezanne, you have enough to cope with for now. Lessons in grammar can wait."

"What dat dere *grammer*? Lak a ol' lady?"

She shook her head, smiled, but didn't answer.

After a moment, I said, "What dat wide Missouri, Aunty? Dat a ribber, lak Shenandoah?"

"Yes, it's a river."

I looked at her keenly. "River?"

"Yes. River."

"Not ribber."

"Not ribber."

I screwed up my face in thought. "You t'ink I kin larn dat? To talk lak you does?"

"Of course."

"When?"

"Gradually. But you will learn. You're a most intelligent boy."

"I *is?*"

"You are."

"Oh. I *are.*"

"No, no. You would say 'I am.' "

"Why I say I yam, when you say I are?"

For the first time, Tamar appeared baffled. "Cezanne," she said at last, "suppose you just pay attention to how I speak, to the words I use, listen to how they sound. In time my way of speaking will—will *seep* into you. You are young enough still to be imitative of language."

"How young is I?"

"I'm not sure. What do you think?"

"Lessee . . . I'se twelb. Jes' decide on dat dis secon'."

"All right. Twelve is a good age, and seems about right for you. Maybe you aren't quite—but it will serve."

Studying her mouth, I said, "Twel-*veh?*"

"More like *twelve*. One syllable. One sound, that is."

"Twelve," I said, heavy on the *v* sound.

"Much better. So, you are a twelve-year-old boy. We've got that settled."

"White folks, dey knows to de *day* how old dey is. Hab parties."

"They certainly do."

"Seems lak we mought could know sumpin' lak dat too. How ol' we is." I gave no thought to a *party* for such as we.

"Seems so."

"You know how ol' you is?"

"No. Sort of—forty, maybe."

"Dat a good age?"

"It'll do, till another comes along. Maybe—maybe next week I'll be thirty-four! *There's* an advantage for you. Pick any age you like, be it for as long as you want, then go forward or backwards."

"Pick a name, too," I said excitedly. "Lak Mam 'n' me did fer me. Miss Mady, she done name Shenandoah. You knowed dat?"

"No. But it's a fine name for a horse."

"Cain't t'ink Missouri'd be fine fer a hoss. I'd name a *mule* Missouri."

"Come along now, Cezanne, we must be on our way."

I sigh sometimes, and I smile, recalling that picnic, that conversation, that woman. It was, of course, the chief day of my existence, when I left the life of slavery behind me, and began—only began—to leave behind me, too, the speech of slavery.

Had no notion where, certainly not how far, I was to go, but was on my way with a hero.

Appellation: Tamar.

When we resumed our march, leaving the creek behind us, we heard hounds baying in the far distance, heard them yelp in indecision. After a bit their voices grew faint and were gone.

On we went. On and on, one foot, the other foot, on and on, one foot, the other foot.

I thought the sun was melting, that it had spread like pale molasses till it filled the sky and dripped down to heat the rough pasture grass we plodded through, grass thick with burdock, stinging thistles, biting and buzzing insects. When a rabbit leaped suddenly across my path, I squealed in fright. By late afternoon, I was thirsty, itchy, sweating, aching all over, tired beyond anything I'd ever felt before.

"Aunty," I said, stopping in my tracks. "Kin we jes' lay yere fer a spell? Jes' a li'l while?"

"Not yet," she said sternly. "After today, we will travel at night until we reach Maryland, guiding ourselves by the North Star. Just now we *must* put all the distance we can between that place and us. We must get to the woods over there and hide."

"Woods?" I said faintly. "Whar?"

Tamar pointed across a stretch of field that looked miles long. In the distance, in the shimmering air, a stand of trees was visible.

"We gotta walk all dat way?" I moaned.

"And many *many* a mile more, Cezanne, before we

get to the Freedom Land. Make up your mind to it. You are only at the start of a long, long, long march."

"Oh, Aunty—I jes' cain't. Leab me yere t' die." I sank to the ground, arms clasped over my head.

When I looked up, Tamar was striding across the pasture. I waited for her to look back, but she just kept walking.

"Meaner nor Blade hisself, y'all!" I shouted, stumbling up. "You'se a crool mean womans!"

Hours later, in the underbrush of the woods, I was permitted to sleep briefly.

When she woke me, Tamar portioned out the second halves of the fish and corn bread we'd eaten earlier, leaving three fish and three cakes in the blanket bundle. She found mushrooms for us, and the moisture in them relieved our thirst somewhat.

Tamar, like many another country woman, knew the properties—healthful and harmful—of growing things. Which roots, berries, leaves or bark of trees would soothe internal afflictions, aid wounds to heal, and which would have effects quite opposite. She could distinguish between mushrooms delicious and safe to eat and those that would send us to kingdom come in a hurry.

"Up now," she said, when it seemed to me we'd barely got down.

Groaning, I obeyed. I knew she'd not walk off and leave me, as she'd pretended to do earlier, but knew too that our only hope lay in pressing forward as hard and as fast as we could, no matter that I felt crackboned with fatigue.

Tamar pointed up through a clearing in the trees to what she said was the North Star. "That will be our guide."

"We gwine folla dat dere hebbenly body?"

"That's what Harriet Tubman said she did. After several trips, of course, she knew the way by heart, all the stopping places, the safe places, the dangerous places. She knew it all. Never lost a passenger."

"Whass dat? Passenger?"

"A person she was leading to freedom on the Underground Railroad."

"Oh, Lawd! I sho' cain't wait to get on dat dere train 'n' set *down*. When we gonna get dere?"

"Cezanne! I *told* you. No. I did not. I recollect

now. I started to explain, but left off. See here, you have to understand that the Underground Railroad is not a railroad that runs on tracks."

"What *do* it run on?"

"It isn't a *train* at all."

"A railroad dat ain't a train?" I asked, wondering how I was supposed to understand that.

"Someone started *calling* it the Underground Railroad, when people began to lead slaves out of the South to free states. They called them—the runaways—'passengers,' and the places that hid them 'stations,' and the people who led them, like Moses, 'conductors.' "

I knew that "Moses" was Harriet Tubman. Every slave knew of Moses, and worshiped her. Every one of us knew how she came again and again, risking her own freedom, into the Egypt's land of Dixie, to lead her people out.

"You and I," Tamar went on, "are heading for the first Underground station, in Maryland, and it's going to be a house, *not* a train. Its location is indicated on this map I have here, that I copied from the map Moses made that time on the dirt floor, and the railroad and the station are on top of the ground, not under it, and that's *all*. Do you understand now?"

"No."

She put her arm over my shoulder. "Well, try. That's all we can do. Try to understand each other. Meanwhile, we'll follow that star. As the shepherds followed their star, long ago."

"S'pose it start rainin'?" I asked. "Cain't see no star iffen it rainin'."

Tamar smiled. "We'll watch for moss on the trees. Moss always grows on the north side of trees. Did you know that, Cezanne?"

"I doan know nuttin'."

"I know something."

"Whass dat?"

"That you are an ornery traveling companion. I forgive you, for now, because you're frightened and tired. But I won't put up with whining indefinitely. Good cheer and manliness had better rise up in your heart, or I'll—"

"What you do, Aunty, iffen good cheer 'n' manliness stay clean t' de bottom an' doan rise up nohow?"

She lifted her hands. "Put up with you, of course. Do I have a choice?"

"I mought could peek down, see iffen a piece a cheer 'n' a mite a manliness is cuddlin' dere, all set t' rise up."

"Wonderful!"

On we went, on and on, for the most part traveling in the dark, feeling our way, grateful when the moon shone. Tamar kept her eye on that steady star. I kept mine on my feet, as I was constantly stumbling over rocks and fallen branches and root systems.

Sometimes, just at dawn's beginning, we would walk along a road, to give ourselves a rest from hacking through the underbrush or slogging through swamps, and then we'd see posters nailed to trees, offering rewards for the return of runaway slaves.

The first time I spied one of them, I stopped and peered at a stencil in the corner of the sheet, showing a little black person running with a stick bundle over his shoulder. Large letters filled most of the space. I could read pretty well by then, but a lot of these words were beyond me.

"What dis yere, Aunty?" I asked. "What dis writin' say?"

Tamar put her hand to her mouth, closed her eyes briefly, then shrugged. "Might as well tell you, now you've noticed them. It's a handbill about a runaway slave. This one describes"—she studied the poster—"one Meshach, says he belongs to R. W. Clavering of Loudoun County, says he's short, very dark complexion, about forty-eight years old and gray-haired. He's a shoemaker. The reward for him is three hundred dollars."

"Dat's *lotsa* dollahs."

"There's been more offered for us." She spoke, then stiffened as though wishing to recover the words.

"Dey got—han'bills 'bout *we*, Aunty?" I said, my heart dropping toewards.

Tamar blew out a breath. "Yes. I saw several, a long way back, and tore them down before you noticed."

"What dey say 'bout we? How much we count fer?"

"What difference does it make?" she said crossly. Then, as I continued to stare at her, "A thousand dollars for me, five hundred for you. The posters said that I'm an unusually tall, bad-tempered, dark-complected woman, good cook, about thirty years old, and that you are a small boy about ten or eleven,

83

lightish skin and good with horses. That we are probably together."

(For Harriet Tubman, by the time she had done her work, leading her three hundred passengers to freedom, later serving behind Confederate lines as a scout and spy for the Union Army, the price on her gallant head was up to forty thousand dollars. Dead or alive. *There's* a horrible expression for you, American as apple pie. They wanted great Moses, quick or dead, but they never laid a hand on her. She lived to a good old age despite them.)

I swallowed hard, looked again at the little running black person on the handbill.

"Hope dis yere Meshach doan git cotched for no t'ree hunner' dollahs."

"I hope he doesn't and we don't, at any price."

Tearing the poster from the tree, she ripped it into pieces and scattered them in the bushes.

"You t'ink dey mought could cotch we dis far fum de plantation, Aunty?"

"I think we'd better get back in the woods. Stay off roads altogether."

*   *   *

We crossed from Virginia into Maryland four days later, in a heavy rainfall, just after dark. I would not, naturally, have been aware that we were in a different state, as there were no border guards or guideposts. Tamar said she knew it from the map she kept consulting, the map Moses had drawn for those who wished to follow her road to freedom.

"Dis *Mary*land a slave place too?" I asked miserably.

"It is. We have to get to Pennsylvania before we're free. And even then—"

I stared at her, wordless. It seemed that the cheer and manliness she'd somehow kept awakening in me during long nights of walking, days of hiding in woods and marshes, were about spent. I'd got over being desperately tired in body, but thought I could actually *see* my courage flopping at my feet like a small wet animal.

"Ebben den—*what?*" I asked at length.

"Cezanne, please. Help me. Be stronger, if you can."

Perhaps it was that she'd never sounded helpless before, perhaps the courage I'd thought moribund had found its second spark of life. Whatever the reason,

I took her hand and said, "Aunty, I'se gwine—" I stopped, then went on. "I'se *going* t' be strong as strong." My "ing" and my *g*'s were heavily stressed.

She squeezed my hand tight, and said, "Cezanne, you're learning! Didn't I say you would?"

Filled with emotion and joy at the thought that I could, indeed, overcome the language of the slave, I met her smiling gaze with a drenched smile of my own. "So. Now you kin tell me what all you started to say, den stopped."

She pondered, nodded, said flatly, "They passed a law, they call it the Fugitive Slave Act. It says that runaways, like us, if we're caught, must be returned to our 'owners.' "

"Ebben in Penns—in dat—*that*—place we s'posed to be free in, lak you say we'se gwine—we *going*—to be free?"

"Even there. I don't believe—I won't believe—that Northern people would chain us, send us back, for *money*. But the truth is that everywhere there are those who will do anything for money. And that *is* a law, so they could say they were being good citizens, and now you know."

"Who made dat dere law?" I said angrily.

"The government, probably."

"Gov'mint? Dat lak a overseer, lak Blade?"

"More like Clayburn and Blade mixed together."

There was a picture to make me shudder. "So, what we gwine—going—to do?"

"Go on, of course. Find the first station on the Underground Railroad. It's right here in Maryland, and not far, not very far, Cezanne. We can make it."

We had long since finished the herring and corn cakes and were living on berries, mushrooms, roots that Tamar said were safe to eat but tasted bitter, black walnuts that we'd found growing wild. They were exceedingly hard to crack and stained our clothes and hands, but were delicious to eat. We'd caught a few little fish and eaten them raw, as we dared not light a fire to cook them over.

Our clothes were torn, dirty, stuck with burdocks and thistles, limp from rains. Tamar had discarded the blankets when they'd got too soggy to protect us, and carried only her knife and the Bible wrapped in oilskin.

So we stumbled on in fear and hope, looking for the first landmark, the first station, on the Freedom

Road that Moses had indicated on her guide to those who came after her.

A hundred—actually two or three—miles later, Tamar put her hand on my shoulder, and we stopped, peering through the rain toward a white farmhouse where soft light glowed at the windows.

"That's it," she whispered unsteadily. "That's the one Mrs. Tubman said is the first station across the Maryland border. There's the big chinaberry trees to either side of the gate, and the white fence, and the cow weathervane atop the barn. See—there's a light at the window, Cezanne! We are here! We have *found* it."

I gulped. "When Moses mak dat dere map?" I asked. "Long time past? Mebbe dis *ain't* a—a station no mo'."

Sounding really angry, Tamar said, "*Must* you be so intelligent? Do I have to have *all* the blind faith for *both* of us?"

"Oh no, Aunty. I mean, I doan mean to be *in-telli*—"

"Hush up, Cezanne! You annoy me, and I don't like that. And stop calling me Aunty. I am Tamar, understand?"

"Yes'm."

"Yes—what?"

"Yes'm—Tamar," I said, wrinkling my nose. "Tamar," I repeated dutifully.

She clucked and pulled me briefly close. "I'm sorry. I shouldn't snap at you. Look here—I am going up to that house and knock at the door. You wait until I am sure it's safe."

"No!" I yelped. "No way I cain't do dat, Aunty! I gotta be wit' you. I cain't stay out yere in the rain by my ownsel', in *no* way. I—"

She put her hand on my mouth. "All right. We'll go together. But let me do the talking, Cezanne."

I thought it funny of her to say that, since she knew that I found it difficult to speak aloud to most grown-ups, and would have no tongue at all, confronted with strange white people.

The simple sad fact was that, confronted with what might be the first haven on our desperate journey, we were facing, too, the fear that it might prove to be no such thing.

We walked slowly across the wet grass, the rain in our faces, opened the gate, crept up the walk to the door. There, after a long moment's wait, Tamar drew a deep breath, glanced down at me, faced forward, and knocked.

The door opened. A tall bearded man stood there, the light of the parlor behind him.

"Come," he said, and drew us inside, to the warmth, to the light, to a fire in the hearth and the smell of baking. Drew us into safety.

A young woman in a gray dress, white muslin cap on her head, white muslin scarf about her neck, rose from a rocker by the fire and came forward, her hands outstretched.

"Oh, do come in," she said. "Thee is most welcome," she said to Tamar, then smiled down at me. "Welcome to thee, too, little brother. Our home is thy home, what we have is thine."

It is wonderful what warmth, firelight, kind words, can do for even the most wretched beings. Surely more for them than for those already safe from weather and fear and hunger? To Tamar and me, close to starvation, undone with exhaustion, our clothes drenched and filthy, that welcome from people we had never seen before was, to us, a sign from God Himself that we would prevail.

Unwilling to move further into the shining, spotless parlor, we stood just inside the door, speechless, shivering, overcome.

"Please, please," the young woman said again, "come in. Sit near the hearth while I prepare a supper for thee." She smiled—oh, so sweetly, so sweetly. "I am sure a bite of supper will not come amiss?"

Tamar said faintly, "No, no. We cannot. Everything—everything is so *clean*, and we . . ." she finished lamely, looking down first at herself, then at me.

We gazed in awe at the room, at its gleaming yellow wood floors and white embroidered curtains, at painted china oil lamps casting a glow over chairs and tables that seemed in themselves to be hospitable. A small piano, with candles in brackets, stood in one corner.

I had never seen, could in no way have imagined, a place of such cleanliness and harmony.

I've long known that it was, in truth, a small, immaculate, sparely furnished farmhouse, but that night it seemed to me surely akin to those illusory palaces in France that Mam had conjured up during nights in the windowless Virginia slave cabin.

My heart hammered at my skinny chest as one part

of me believed what I saw, and another part held that I was making it up, that such a place, such people were found only in dreams.

"Look at us!" Tamar burst out. "We are wet and ragged. We're covered with *mud*."

"No more of this!" said the man, taking each of us by the hand. "Ezra!" he called, and a boy a little older than I came from the kitchen. "Ezra, please to put a bucket of water on the stove to heat, so that our guests may wash. And I, Mother," he said, turning to the young woman, who was clearly his wife, "shall rummage in the wardrobe for clothing whilst thee prepares a thanksgiving meal."

He added, to us, "For we are thankful that God has guided thy footsteps to our door."

We stood by the fire, grateful past words for its warmth, its leaping cheer, but Tamar refused to let us sit until, some time later, we had bathed and were in new—new to us—clothes. Tamar wore a man's coat and pants, which suited her height and air of command, and I, for the first time in my life, was in woolen britches, a knitted sweater, and shoes, all contributed by Ezra. The shoes felt strange and uncomfortable, but I would not have said so for anything in the world, with my heart full of such melting gratitude for the manner in which we had been taken in and comforted and promised food and shelter and a wagon ride to the next station, when the man, John Forrest, thought it safe to go.

The kitchen table, spread with a white cloth, had blue-and-white plates arranged on it. Against the wall was a black cookstove with nickel handles. There were open shelves of preserved fruits and vegetables, other shelves with blue-and-white dishes tidily disposed upon them. Here too the windows had white curtains.

We sat together—three white people, two black— five strangers behaving as friends. They told us that they were members of a religious body, the Society of Friends. Called, sometimes, Quakers, these were friends to mankind in the deep, the true sense of the word.

John Forrest said grace, and his wife, whose name was Hannah, said we were to call her so. She set before us the most glorious meal of my entire life. None before, none since, has equaled it. There was fried chicken, biscuits so light they floated in the hand, butter, relishes, a variety of vegetables. And a pie. A rhubarb pie, with a sugary flaky crust, a rich, tart, juicy filling, and a *taste* . . . How can I describe the taste of that, the inaugural pie of my existence?

I say that the miraculous food, the manna supplied to the Israelites and delivered to them by invisible hands in the wilderness where they wandered, was rhubarb pie, baked in a Quaker oven.

I had never handled fork or spoon, though I had seen such implements when visiting Mam or Tamar in the kitchen of Gloriana. Slave children ate solid food with their fingers, scooped mush from troughs with oyster shells. We did not have dishes. There I sat, staring in bewilderment at food on a plate, at the tools with which I was supposed to get at it.

Licking my lips, I glanced around the table—at Ezra, already eating, at Mr. and Mrs. Forrest, who were waiting for us, then at Tamar, who put her hand on mine before she picked up her fork. Pushing it under some green beans, she lifted them to her mouth. It looked easy, but when I attempted to do likewise, the beans fell off my fork. Blinking back tears, I tried to smile. Then Hannah (I never brought myself to call her by name during the brief time we were in their house but have said it to myself many times over in the years since) said, "Chicken is to be picked up in our fingers. The vegetables will set nicely in the bowl of a spoon."

She scooped up a spoonful of beans, smiled at me, then took a chicken leg and began to chew it heartily. In a moment, I followed suit, and presently was eating the meal of my life.

Manna in my wilderness.

Supper over, dishes washed and put back in their place, Tamar said that she and I, with blessings forever upon them, would be on our way.

"I fear to bring some danger upon you, should a patty-roller or slave catcher discover our whereabouts."

"Nay," said John Forrest, "they shall not find thee here."

"But surely you have sheltered runaways before us. Your farm is on Harriet Tubman's map. They must suspect you."

"We know about the map. But no one has yet betrayed us, and with God's help, we shall continue our work until this nation is delivered from the unspeakable curse of slavery."

Tamar gave him an incredulous glance. "You believe that will happen?"

"I do. It may be a terrible deliverance, but it will come. God will not tolerate such inhumanity, such grievous injustice to His black children, indefinitely."

Ezra and I exchanged glances, and as if we had spoken I knew our thoughts were identical. Why had God tolerated it to begin with, why had He let it continue? Being children, we left the question unspoken.

For me, it is a question unanswered to this day.

At the bidding, almost the direction, of John and Hannah Forrest, we agreed to stay the night and the following day.

"Thee must rest," Hannah said. "We have a small attic room above these, with beds, where travelers have stayed before and shall again."

"Tomorrow, after dark," said John, "I shall take thee in my wagon to the next stop. It is best to travel by night. Following a day spent there, thy way must be on foot until thee reaches Pennsylvania. In Philadelphia, at an address I shall give thee, is a Vigilance Committee. They will assist thee in thy trip onward to Canada, as even in free states no person of color is safe in this country, owing to the infamous Fugitive Slave Act."

"Is not Philadelphia called the City of Brotherly Love?" Tamar inquired, in that flat tone she sometimes used.

"It is. I am loath to say that only white brethren are sufficiently loved so as to be able—say, to ride inside on a streetcar."

"And where, pray, do we *culluds* ride?"

John's lips tightened. "On a platform just behind the horses."

"Pay a smaller fare?"

"No."

"I see. So. We go on, to Canada."

"It seems the wisest course."

That was the first I heard of Canada. I suppose Tamar and the Forrests had discussed plans while I was on the little back porch, taking the first warm bath of my life, in a copper tub, with a cake of *soap*. With that bath, I felt exhilarated, as if I were washing away my entire former life. Not a feeling that could last, but one I have not forgotten.

97

Later, John said, "I noticed, Cezanne, when thee was in the tub, a harmonica on the washstand. Canst thee play on it?"

"Oh, yessuh. I larned fum Cupid, de blacksmit'. He gib it me when we run off."

"We could have a hymn, could we not, Father?" said Hannah, seating herself at the little piano, and smiling at me. "Dost know this, Cezanne?" She began to play, softly, a hymn I was happy to find I did know.

So we played together, and all sang except myself, busy blowing on Cupid's music maker.

The little wheel run by faith,
And the big wheel run by the Grace of God.
There's a wheel in the wheel, O Lord!
Way in the middle of the air!

All these things—the bath, the meal, the fork and spoon, the talk of Canada, the making of music and singing with white folks—were not the only initiations of that night for me. There was the attic room, where five beds stood in a row. Each had white sheets, a colorful quilt, and a *pillow.*

"Aunty," I said, when we were upstairs together, and I had removed the painful shoes. "What dem dere t'ings?" I was close to frenzy at too much unfamiliar kindness, too many strange comforts. Even my speech, which I'd been proudly improving upon, now seemed to revert to the slave quarter.

"These are beds, Cezanne. Surely you know what beds are."

I'd heard the word. "We s'posed to put oursel's down 'pon dem?"

"That's what beds are for. To lay yourself upon. You pull the sheet and quilt up for coverlets, and off you go to slumberland."

I picked up a pillow. "What dis fer? It sho' *soft*."

"To put your head on. It makes sleep come sooner."

"Dat de trut'?" I said, holding the pillow to my chest. "I doan need no sich fer gwine t' sleep. I'se asleep now, wit' my eyes open."

"Then take off your nice new clothes, and get under the covers and *close* your eyes. You'll sleep better that way."

But sleep hovered beyond my reach.

In the clean and narrow cot, stunned to find myself lying *above* the floor, my head on a pillow, I listened to a familiar nighttime *wheep-poor-weel* coming from the woods, from some cousin to a bird now surely singing in the woods around Gloriana. Once there came, from a nearby crossroads no doubt, the long wavering whistle of a train passing in the dark.

"Dat de Freedom Train, comin' fer to carry we to Canada," I murmured to myself, singsong, then whispered, "Aunty, you sleepin'?"

"No, Cezanne."

"Whass gwine hoppen to we?"

"We go on, until we reach freedom."

"We sho' 'nuff goin' to dat dere Canada?"

"We are, sure enough."

"We be safe dere, sho' 'nuff? *Sure enough*," I corrected myself, concentrating on each syllable.

"Canada is an English country, Cezanne. Nobody there can be or own a slave. There *is* no slavery, in Canada."

I pondered on such an unlikely land. Such a country would be more than Freedom Land. It would be, in truth, the Promised Land, the one God offered to all of us—any old color allowed in.

"What we gwine do in Canada, Aunty? How we

gwine git food 'n' a roof? We gwine lib—*live*—in the woods, lak—like—we bin doin'?"

"I am going to get a job, like regular people. I shall of course be a cook. For wages."

"Whass dat?"

"Money that I work for, and earn, and keep all for us. Don't have to hand it over to any 'owner.' Work for it, keep it."

"*Fancy dat*," I said. It was an expression of Miss Mady's and seemed to come in handy right then. "An' me? What I be gwine do?"

"You are going to be my family. You will be my nephew, and when I become a cook, I'll explain that you come with me or I go elsewhere. Will you be my nephew, Cezanne?"

Tears trickled down my cheeks. "I'se happy to be dat, an' you—your—famb'ly."

"Good. Then you can go on calling me Aunty. One problem out of the way," she said, yawning.

"Dese berry—very—nice folkses, ain't dey, Aunty?"

"Oh, they are far far more than nice. I expect if there are saints on earth, people like the Forrests would qualify."

"Talks funny, doan dey?"

Tamar gave a little snort of laughter.

"Yes'm," I said, yawning in turn. "But I'se gwine larn—learn—how t' . . ."

The next I knew, it was the following day.

In the forenoon John Forrest, in overalls and a broad-brimmed black hat, worked in the field behind the house, turning up the earth with a mule and plow. Tamar worked with Hannah in the house, while Ezra and I repaired to the barn and sorted apples for drying.

"Hab dere bin lotsa folks lak we stay here wit' y'all?" I asked him.

"Oh, yes. We are grateful that our home is on the route of the Underground Railroad. God has been good to us in this, as in so much."

There was no question of that.

"Las' night, when your daddy say God gwine stop slavery in de nation, did you wonder why He let it go on in de firs' place? I t'ink I seed you wonder dat."

Ezra looked uncomfortable. "I suppose I did. But it is not for us to question the ways of the Creator. In the end, all will be made clear to thee and to me."

"I s'pose," I said doubtfully.

He and his family had been unhesitatingly good to

a pair of runaway slaves—strangers, and very possibly a danger to them. They did this again and again, in God's name. It would be, I thought confusedly, ungrateful to question him about why God had ordered things so that *he* woke up white and unafraid every morning, while *I* arose black and frightened.

"I use-ta t'ink de Underground Railroad was unnerneat' de groun'," I told him. "Runnin' down dere, hootin' an' hollerin' an' smokin' till it bust into de Freedom Lan'—'cept I dint know where *dat* was. Still doan know."

"I used to think that too. That it was in a tunnel under the earth."

I smiled with pleasure. "You did? Sho' 'nuff?"

Ezra nodded. "Dost mind if I draw thy attention to an oddity?"

With no idea of what an oddity might be, I assured him I would not mind at all.

"Well . . . when thee said 'Underground Railroad,' thee pronounced it correctly, but then a moment later thee said 'unnerneat'!"

"Dat an oddity?" I asked.

"Well, not an important one."

"I'se gwine t' larn t' talk real good. Tak—take—

103

time, Tamar say, but I'se gwine larn, fer sartin. Jes' tak time," I repeated.

"I am sure thee will end by speaking as well as we do."

I accepted that, wondering if I'd say "thee" and "thy" as he did, thinking I wouldn't mind at all.

For a while we sorted apples in silence. Then I said curiously, "Where you t'ink is de Promise' Lan' at?"

"For you?"

Taken aback, I realized he thought we'd end up in different parts of heaven.

John Forrest, coming into the barn at that moment, to get a tool perhaps, heard us, and came to our side.

"Ezra," he said sadly. "Oh, *Ezra*. The Promised Land is promised to *all* of us. God takes no account of color in His heaven."

"Why does He take account of it here, then?" Ezra said daringly, then looked—not alarmed but as if he couldn't believe he had questioned his own father.

John closed his eyes, lifted his head, put his hands briefly to his lips. "Thee must not quiz the Lord,

Ezra. Nor"—he glanced at me—"must you, little brother. He moves in mysterious ways, but He is a benevolent God, and we must trust in Him and in His heaven."

"I does," I said truthfully. I always had, still do, perhaps.

But I've come to have reservations that, unlike Ezra, I'd not then dreamed of. Reservations about the nature of God's heaven, about the Land of His Promise, about just how different the ground rules are there than here.

CHAPTER THREE

In the evening, after another simple, wonderful meal, we said good-bye to Hannah, who gave Tamar a basket of food and me a bundle of clothing for our trip north.

She and Ezra stood at the door as we went to the barn, where John Forrest had a horse and wagon waiting. We lay in the back and he covered us with blankets, then arranged bushel baskets of fruits and vegetables around us.

"I fear it will prove a dark and bumpy journey, and a lengthy one," he said. "If it is necessary that I stop, thump on the boards, but if thee canst, wait until we reach the farm of Dorcas Miller in Damascus. We should be there by dawn. Dorcas will house and feed thee tomorrow, and set thy course to Pennsylvania, a walk of some fifty miles."

"For us," said Tamar, "a stroll. Is that not so, Ce-zanne?"

"Oh, *yes'm*," I said.

That Pennsylvania, a free state, should lie a wagon trip and a fifty-mile hike away seemed to me the stuff of dreams. Indeed, I fell sound asleep on the hard boards of the iron-wheeled wagon as it bumped and trundled through the night.

Our long—in every sense of the word—journey from Virginia and slavery to Canada and freedom took place about eighty years ago, and much is blurred now in my recollection, though I thought at the time never to forget a moment.

But the Forrest household is to me so clear, so dear, that I feel I could walk through that gate between the chinaberry trees and up to that door today, and knock, and find Hannah and John stretching their hands out to welcome us in.

When the war was over, I thought I would go back to Maryland and do that. After I went to Texas to find Mam. That had to come first. But, as the poet says, ". . . knowing how way leads on to way, I doubted if I should ever come back—"

I never returned to the Forrests' door. I think of them, wonder how long they lived, whether they were caught and punished or continued their saintly work until the war was over, and then knew peace. I muse upon Ezra. Months after we were in Canada, when war had broken out in the States, Tamar got a letter from Hannah Forrest in which she told, with troubled restraint, how Ezra had run off to become a drummer boy in the Union Army. He would be prepared to carry, he said in his farewell note, a musket if they gave him one.

"It is against all that we believe in, all we tried to teach him," Hannah wrote, "and there is nothing we can do now but pray for him, and for all who are going to suffer in this terrible conflict. Ezra said that it is wrong of us to pray for both sides. We cannot do otherwise."

The letter was longer, but I can't remember more now than the fact of Ezra's action, and the suffering it caused his strong, gentle parents.

We reached the farm belonging to Dorcas Miller, where she too took us into the kindly safety of her home, then told us the route to Pennsylvania, to

Philadelphia. Five days later, exhausted, we stumbled up worn and splintery stairs to the shelter of the Vigilance Committee. We had not eaten for two days, our feet were bleeding, our clothes again filthy.

William Still, one of the few, the very very few, black men of wealth in America, was in the office that evening. He was a thriving coal merchant and head of the Philadelphia station of the Underground Railroad. For years he had been leading a fight against the segregated streetcars that John Forrest had told us of. Three years, and still our people rode behind the horses, no matter the weather, no matter that they paid the same fare as white riders. Mr. Still's handsome face was stern and unsmiling. To fight and to fail again and again, when what you are asking is not favors but justice, would sober the cheeriest being. He had been striving for a long and bitter time.

He had coffee and sandwiches brought to us, listened intently as we told him of our trials, of our trip, then discussed plans for our emigration to Canada.

A member of the Vigilance Committee arranged for us to stay in a boardinghouse, and got work for Tamar in a laundry. I found a job as ostler in a nearby stable. We never attempted to ride a streetcar. Even in "free" Pennsylvania the Fugitive Slave Act made the lives of such as we a constant risk, so we stayed just long enough to earn money to get our clothes cleaned, add some articles suited to a northern climate, buy boat tickets, and pay for board in Canada until we found work. Then, again with Mr. Still's help, we went to Pittsburgh, riding Jim Crow on the train.

It wasn't a law yet, but Jim Crow was how we rode.

Jim Crow?

That form of segregation was not yet an actual statute, but was everywhere the practice of the time. The law itself was passed in 1875, by Tennessee. The rest of the white South hastened to make legal a standard of separation admirably designed to settle a vexing question:

"What is the black person's 'place,' and how do we keep him there?"

What did they conclude—by decree—was our place?

Why, outside.

Outside, looking in.

Outside, riding in the rain behind the horses.

Outside, barred from entry to all "places" the white man considered his.

It is no longer a law. But now, more than half a century later, it might as well be. We still live by Jim Crow in the South, and there are those in the North who'd like mighty well to see us all back there.

Except—we won't go. That's something they will have to understand.

We won't go Jim Crow no mo', see?

Anyway, not in Chicago.

Someday—I may not see the day, but it will come— in the North, the South, the West, the East, all over this nation, we shall ride and drink and eat and hang our hats wherever the white folks ride and drink and eat and hang theirs.

If we want to.

After Pittsburgh, we walked the rest of the way, north to Erie, where we were to take the boat to Ontario. With a cardboard suitcase (a mighty step up from the blanket bundle) containing warm clothes and Tamar's Bible, we made our way to the boat landing.

I shan't while I live forget my first sight of the steam paddle-wheeler *Victoria,* the magic craft that would bear us across the lake to Canada and unqualified liberty. It loomed there at dockside, graceful, immaculate, with sparkling windows brightly curtained, shining brass fittings. A brass bell hung outside the wheelhouse, wherein I spied a powerful figure. It was the pilot himself, a huge man standing at a great wheel, uniform trim, cap jaunty, ready for the signal to get under way.

I thought to myself—would not have dared say it to Tamar—that *God* might look like a ship's pilot, all by Himself in a wheelhouse high above the dock, above the land and the luminous, lifting waters. Above the earth, and all of us people waiting.

We had left Virginia in late spring. Now it was October. We had never before felt the peppery winds of autumn on our faces, or seen leaves swirling in air like rooster feathers. We had never seen or dreamed of such a ship as this, which now we were, our very selves, about to board.

Dazzled, elated, staring about us in triumph and trepidation, we gripped each other's hands tightly.

Posing as father and son, we stood on the dock while the boat was got ready to leave. Tamar wore the suit that John Forrest had given her. I, accustomed but not resigned to shoes, was wearing Ezra's, also his woolen britches and cap and warm knitted sweater.

Suddenly I noticed two men who eyed us and begun whispering to each other. Sidling close, keeping behind some large crates, I overheard words that sent me into a spell of terrified shivering.

"Looks like 'em, sure enough," the first man said.

"You're loco. The reward is for a female and a boy, and they orter be runnin' skeert. Them two don't look a bit—hey! Where'd the boy go? He was there a minute ago."

"Anythin' says a woman tryin' to escape slavery cain't get herself up in a fella's duds? I say them two is the escapees that we heard about las' summer that's been on the run all this time and still is wanted. Prob'ly been he'ped by those crazy abolitionists. I say less take 'em."

"They mought be free, you think of that, maybe?"

"Them posters say they ain't free, and I aim to collec' that whole bloomin' two thousan' fer returnin' 'em to Virginny, free or not free makes no never-mind."

Behind the crates, swallowing against sickness, I had time to think that the price on us had gone up somewhat. Why were we so valuable to Clayburn? As examples? For Tamar's cooking, or my way with horses?

Oh, but to get this far, only to be caught and chained and dragged back and probably sold downriver as a lesson to would-be runaways! To be so close to freedom and miss it! I thought I would jump in the lake first, and try to swim to freedom. Except I couldn't swim. Then *drown*, I thought . . .

Scuttling back to Tamar's side, I tugged at her hand. Trying to whisper but sounding shrill, I said, "Aunty, dose mens dere—behin' you, doan look, jes' lissen—dey is *slave* cotchers, an' says dey gonna *tak* us fer de *re*ward, thass done gone up t' two t'ousan' dollahs. What we gwine *do*, Aunty?"

Tamar closed her eyes. A tear trickled from each shut lid. "And you were coming along so nicely with your pronunciation," she said. For the first time since I'd known her she sounded defeated. "Cezanne, I don't know what to do now. Unless we yell aloud to the people and tell what those men are up to. If anyone would *listen* to us. Or maybe help them, instead of us. I don't know what to do," she said again, her shoulders slumping.

As we stood there in a panic, unable to make a move to help ourselves, a man in a frock coat and high beaver hat, carrying a beautiful gold-knobbed cane, approached us. "I see you are troubled. May I be of assistance?" he asked, in an accent I'd not heard before.

We stared at him in open-mouthed silence.

"I overheard the lad," he went on, "and wish to say that nobody—not those two ruffians, not *anyone* while I am on the scene—is going to return *anyone* to slavery."

Turning as the two "ruffians" shuffled toward us, he inquired coldly, "Your business?"

"Wal—you see, sor—" said the vociferous one, ducking his head in a servile way, "We is terrible oneasy about your *personal* safety, 'cause of bein' downright *con*vinced that these two which jus' now engaged you in *con*versation are a pair of dastardly runaways that kilt a entire fine Virginny famb'ly afore fleein' the place where they was born and bred and treated real good, real good."

"What gives you this idea, pray?"

"They—wal, yer honor, they *looks* 'xactly like the scoundrelly murderers what we've been hired to folly 'n' return to their rightful owners and justful punishment. We're *Pinkertons*," he said, as if a light had gone on in his brain, revealing, in some murky corner, a telling ploy.

"This is not slave country, fellow," said the elegant man, advancing on them, waving his cane from side to side as if to sweep them into the water. "In any case," he added, "this is my coachman"—he indicated Tamar—"and this his son. Now—take yourselves off, and be quick about it!"

One of the men scooted, but the first stood his ground a bit longer. Narrowing his eyes, he said, "Coachman, yer worship? Where's his lib'ry?"

"I see no call to answer your insolence. However—to be rid of you—my regular coachman has taken sick, and I have not had opportunity to purchase livery for—for Maury, here. Now—off, off! Before I call a real policeman!"

When he'd gone, the man looked at us and said, "I fancy you'll have no more trouble with that pair."

"Master," said Tamar, "I cannot think of words in the world to thank you."

"No 'master,' please. My name is Ramsey. Yours, of course, is not Maury. It was all I could think to say on the spur of the moment. Jim Maury is my coachman, and has indeed taken a turn. I trust not serious. He's in the carriage there."

He gestured toward a black brougham with gilt trim and fittings, hitched to a beautiful gray mare. The outfit was drawn up on the dock, ready to be the first carriage on board the steamboat.

"Maury is inside," Mr. Ramsey went on, "and I have driven the thing myself some fifteen miles to get here. I am on my way back to Ontario, and am in haste to have him seen to." He added, with an easy smile and a glance down at his clothing, "A proper sight I must be, up there in the driver's seat, in my *lib'ry*."

"Well, Mr. Ramsey," said Tamar, "there is no way we shall every forget your—gallantry."

"You are not, of course, despite your garb, a man."

"No. Nor is Cezanne"—she put a hand on my shoulder—"my son, though as close to me as a son could be."

"You too are on your way to Canada?"

"We are." With a searching glance at him, Tamar said, "I tell you honestly that we *are* the pair those slave catchers were after."

"But did not slaughter an entire fine Virginia family before running off?" he said with a smile.

"All were alive and well when we—departed. It's possible that Massa Clayburn expired with rage when he found us gone," Tamar said in an offhand way. "Still, there is a large sum offered for us. It's a tempting situation for many men. I think that only in Canada will we be free of fear."

"You are very well spoken," said Mr. Ramsey, then looked annoyed with himself.

Tamar said dryly, "People do not expect those of my complexion to be 'well spoken.'"

"My apologies. That was crass of me."

I had listened, dumbfounded, to this exchange, as the gentleman in his elegance, Tamar in her frayed man's outfit, conversed as equals. It went beyond the bounds of credence—or at any rate, my credence.

The steamboat whistle sounded, indicating that carriages and passengers might begin to board. Tamar and I turned away, turned back when Mr.

Ramsey said to her, "I wonder—could you by chance drive the brougham? Could you handle the mare? She's biddable, and would not give you trouble."

Tamar hesitated, then said, "I doubt if I could drive a rocking horse, but Cezanne, now—he's young and small, but has the finest way with horseflesh of anyone—black or white, bar none—in Virginia. Just lovely with them, he is."

I could scarcely keep from smiling. Now and then Tamar would come out with a statement like that, as if no one dared doubt her word.

Mr. Ramsey seemed to, for a moment; then he looked at me and said, "Needs must, when the devil drives, eh, Cezanne? Not that you appear to be a devil, but if you feel capable . . ."

I walked over to the mare. She stood with head nicely set, left hind leg cocked while the other three carried her weight. She was resting, but not asleep. I stroked her withers, ran my hand from her forehead to the delicate velvety nostrils.

"Whass her name?" I asked.

"Callie."

"She jes' lubly. Lovely," I corrected myself. It was

a word Tamar favored. "Callie gal, less you 'n' me dribe—drive de peoples to dat dere free land ob—of Canada. You go nice 'n' easy fer me?"

Mr. Ramsey smiled and said to Tamar, "Looks as if I have a coachman for the nonce."

I clambered up to the high driver's seat. Tamar started to follow, but Mr. Ramsey said, "No need of that. Please to sit inside with Maury and me. Have you nursing experience?"

"Some."

"Then perhaps you can give me an idea . . ."

They climbed inside, closed the door, and I, lifting reins and letting them fall, guided Callie onto the boat, my heart thudding with pride, with joy, with disbelief, with—there is no other word for it—*rapture*.

When we were settled aboard, and I had dropped the reins so that Callie would stand, Mr. Ramsey said it would be all right if I went on deck to watch as the *Victoria* churned away from the dock and headed out on the choppy, sun-polished waters of the wide lake. Gulls turned above us, crying like kittens, the great paddle wheel revolved, tossing waterfalls through

121

its blades, and I stood at the front of the boat ("prow," I later learned) and breathed till I thought my very lungs were pumping the ether of freedom.

Freedom!!!!

It was an overnight trip to Port Stanley, Ontario. Mr. Ramsey, of course, had a cabin. Tamar slept inside, in what was called the saloon though no liquor was served there, and Jim Maury remained in the carriage. I stayed on deck, sometimes stretched out on a bench but mostly walking around and around, stopping from time to time to watch the white wake froth and toss in a fan far behind us, then to look up at the sky, atremble with millions, billions, of stars.

Somewhere in *Huckleberry Finn* occurs what seems to me a perfect sentence:

It's lovely to live on a raft.

No way to improve on that. At night, Huck and Jim would loll on their backs, letting the raft float with the current, seeing the light of a candle in a cabin window on the far shore, sometimes hearing a fiddle tune or a song coming over the water from another craft. There they would lie, looking at the stars, wondering whether they were made or had only happened, Jim saying they'd been made, Huck allowing as how they had just happened.

Then Jim says—when I read this years later I caught my breath with the sheer *pleasure* of such a fancy—Jim says, "Maybe the moon could 'a' *laid* them, Huck."

That night on the *Victoria*, too happy, too excited, too apprehensive for sleep, I gazed long at the stars, and knew nought of Huck and Jim. The book was yet to be written, and in any case I could not have read it at that stage of my "education"—scarcely to be called that then.

But the thought of the moon laying those billions and trillions of glittering eggs in her transit across the sky so delights me that I insert the passage here for fear of omitting it later on, through hurry or forgetfulness.

Alone on deck that night, I too speculated about the makeup of stars, and what *I* decided was that God had probably pieced them out of bits left over from halos and things like that.

*　　*　　*

Twice during the hours aboard I went to check on Callie.

In the back of the brougham, outside, was a box containing some luggage, a canvas feed bag, a pail, and a sack of oats. I filled the bag, secured it over her ears, then stood with my hand on her neck, and listened to the sound of those great teeth grinding. When she got to the bottom of the nose bag, tossing it up several times to catch the last morsels, I took the pail out to a water spigot on the deck. After she'd drunk her fill, I cleaned up her droppings, then remained, talking to her quietly, as once I had talked to Shenandoah. I told her about *our* journey, Tamar's and mine, about our long long journey. I told her of the filly I'd left behind me.

"Shenandoah her name was. Nice name. Your name nice too. She a pinto. So purty. Pretty. So pretty. Me 'n' her use-ta ride out 'crost de meadows jes' to gib—give her exercise. Y'all knows how *im*portant it is—exercise fer a hoss. An' times I play her some music. Lak dis—"

Taking Cupid's harmonica from my pocket, I played, softly as I could, an old air he'd taught me about a girl named Sally that someone left behind him. Callie pricked her ears forward, listening. *I'm lonesome since I crossed the hill and o'er the moor and valley. Such lonesome thoughts my heart do fill, since parting with my Shandy—*

Then: *O Shenandoah, I long to hear you. O Shenandoah, I long to see you. Way, hey, I'm bound to leave you* . . .

"Oh, I do miss dat pretty li'l hoss," I said, and put the harmonica away.

Leaning my head against Callie's neck, I cried till my ribs ached. It seemed I had tears for everything I'd ever known. For Mam, who was lost to me. For field hands summoned from sleep—their only release—by the overseer's harsh dawn horn. For whippings and ugly names and brutal words. I wept for the hunger, and the cold, and the chain gangs slogging south to Natchez or New Orleans. Cried because I was afraid I'd never see Mam or Shenandoah or Cupid again. Cried because I didn't know what freedom, lying just across the wide Lake Erie, was to bring us.

I cried because Mam and those field hands and Tamar and I were black and different, and all the others—even the good and the kind—were white and the same.

I cried because there was nothing else I could do.

There was the sound of the carriage door opening and a hand fell upon my shoulder, causing me to jump in alarm.

"No, no," said a hoarse voice. "No need to buck like that. I heard you sobbing your innards out and thought maybe I could help. *Is* there some way I can help?"

Dragging the back of my hand across my mouth, I swallowed hard and said, "Is you Massa Maury?"

"I'm Maury all right. Jim Maury's the name, and I'm no 'massa.' Just Maury, coachman for the Ramseys."

"Y'all got de mis'ry?"

"I sure don't feel good."

"Whyn't you stay in dat dere brum?"

"I just said. I heard you crying. I can't bear to hear a child cry. Let's go out on deck and set a spell."

"Mebbe you git mo' mis'ry doin' dat?"

"Don't see how I could get more. Come along."

On deck, in the light coming from the saloon, I

126

saw a tall, dark-skinned, heavyset man with gray wool hair and beard. He had a voice as deep as Cupid's, husky from whatever ailed him, but he spoke like Tamar, or Mr. Ramsey himself. Spoke as I intended to, as soon as I could manage it.

"Your aunt is a kindly woman," he said.

"She sho' is. Nex' my Mam, she de bes' womans in de whole worl'."

"You ran away together, did you?"

"Oh, yes, Massa. Long time—long time in de pas'. So far gone," I said wearily. "All on it jes' mak me dizzy. I could lay down yere 'n' sleep f'ever."

It was true. All at once my lids and limbs were leaden.

"Lie down," said the deep-voiced man. "Put your head on my lap. Sleep . . ."

Feeling I should resist, since he was sick and I was only tired, I did as he bid. The sun was up when I woke and found him with his head back, mouth open, snoring faintly, but holding me close.

When we docked in Port Stanley, Mr. Ramsey said I was to drive the brougham to his home, Clive Court, some thirty miles distant, and then he would see what arrangements he could make for Tamar and me to get jobs.

I could work with his horses, but he already had a cook. An Irish lady, he said, who wouldn't tolerate a rival in her kitchen. Anyway, Tamar wouldn't work at the bidding of any other cook in the world.

We slept over the stable that night. There was a stable hand there—white—who didn't look happy about having to share his living quarters, even though we were in a separate partition, but Mr. Ramsey simply *looked* him into silence.

Lying in bed, in the dark, as we had that long-ago night in the Forrests' attic, Tamar and I spoke of our lives. Not where we'd been. Where we were going.

"Cezanne," she said, "we are very very lucky. You know that?"

"I sure does, Aunty."

"Good! You said 'sure,' not 'sho'.' "

"I'se—I yam learnin'. Learn*ing*."

"It's not 'I yam.' You must say 'I *am*.' And 'I do,' not 'I does.' But you *are* learning, and I think you're wonderful."

"You does?"

"Do. I *do*."

"Dat's—that's *good*, Aunty."

"Now," she went on, "Mr. Ramsey thinks that among his friends he can find me a position as a cook, and I'll be glad of that. For a while. But my idea—" She stopped and drew a quivery breath. "*My* idea, Cezanne, is to one day go to college and learn to be a teacher!"

"Oh, Aunty! Kin you do dat, all on your ownsel'?"

"I'll have to work, and put aside every penny, for a long time beforehand. But that is what I see ahead for me. As soon as I have saved enough, I could send for you, and maybe you could go to school too. A regular school."

When I hesitated, she said, "Don't *ever* let me force you to say, or to do, anything you don't want to, Cezanne. Your days of being or doing things against your will are over. Do you understand?"

I said, reluctant to go against her, but with no choice, because she had asked me a question that required an answer, "What I sees fer my ownsel', Aunty, is sumpin' to do wit' hosses. I jes' doan see mysel' in no school. I'se—I yam—I *am* sorry to say dis—"

"Oh, my boy, don't be sorry. You can't know how

129

it pleases me to find you strong in your mind. Cezanne, you are *growing*. You are becoming someone who knows himself, and that makes me happy, so happy."

"Dat's good, Aunty, dat's real . . ."

Again I fell asleep in the middle of a sentence.

Mr. Ramsey found a place for Tamar in the kitchen of a friend, living a good distance away. I was taken on as a stable hand at Clive Court. So we were to be separated for the first time in many years.

"It won't be like losing your own mother," she told me, as we sat together on a bench outside the stable, the afternoon before she left. "It won't hurt in the same way at all as that time, Cezanne. Because we will get to see each other, and we'll know where each of us *is,* and what's happening with us."

Though I was finding it hard to face being without her, she was surely right in what she said. It might not be often, but we would contrive to meet. And we were not like Mam and all those others who'd been sold away from each other's presence, from all knowledge of how Fate would choose to handle us.

Mam had sat straight-backed in that wagon, waving to me until the bend in the dirt road took her forever from my sight. Tamar was going to ride several miles away, but I would know where she was. And *there* was all the difference.

"I'll write to you, Cezanne. And you must try to write back."

"Oh, yes'm, I sho'ly—surely I do dat. That."

We sat in silence for a few minutes, and then I said, "Aunty. I got a plan too."

"Besides horses?"

"Maybe wit' dem. Them. When I'se done de—the firs' part."

"What's the first part?"

"First part. *First* I gwine go—I'm go*ing* to go to Texas. Fin' Mam."

"Texas—" She hesitated. "Texas is a very big, an enormous place to try to find someone in."

"Cupid say de same t'ing."

"Alas, Cezanne—we're both right."

"Jes' de same. Thass what—that's what I—gonna do."

"Not yet. You're too young. And Cezanne—they are maybe going to get in a war down there."

"What dey gwine fight 'bout?"

"Some say about *us*. But I don't know—"

"Us! What fer? We ain't doin' nuttin' 'cept what we're tol'. Or," I added, grinning at her, "runnin' off. Dey gwine—gonna get in a war 'cause you 'n' me 'scaped? Ain't *dat* sumpin'."

"The way I heard, two territories, Kansas and Nebraska, or maybe it's Arkansas, are about to become part of the Union—"

"Whass dat? The union?"

"It's the United States of America, where we lived. Virginia's part of it." She waited to see if I had further questions, but I hadn't. I did not, in truth, care what went on in the United States of America, just so long as I wasn't in it.

"The Southern states," Tamar went on, "want to extend slaveholding into Arkansas and Kansas, or maybe it's Nebraska, only it seems they—the Southern states—agreed long ago in a thing called the Missouri Compromise that there wouldn't be slavery in new states that come into the Union, and now they've gone back on their word."

"Why dey do dat?" I said angrily.

"Because we've always been such good business for them, and now there's a law says they can't go get us in Africa anymore, so they—" She stopped with a sick-sounding sigh. "They've taken to *breeding* us, right here—I mean *there*, in the South—so now they've got homegrown slaves that they have to sell. There are people, like William Still and Moses, and a lot of white abolitionists, who want to put a stop to it—"

"A stop to *what?*" I asked miserably.

"Cezanne! To the slave trade. What have I been talking about?"

"I dunno. I got a headache, thass all I know."

"Well, so have I. But I'm trying to explain something important to you. There are those people, the abolitionists, who want to stop the spread of slavery, and other people who want to make it get bigger. So there's maybe going to be a war about it. Do you understand?"

"No."

"Neither do I. But there's one thing I know for sure—*you* can't go traveling to Texas in a country where half of it is getting ready to kill the other half. You might get killed yourself down there. There's a saying goes, 'In the end it makes no difference if I die today or tomorrow, but I prefer tomorrow.' "

"I prefers dat too," I said fervently.

"Naturally. Well—maybe they'll sort it out without a war, but you wait and see before you hightail it to Texas."

"I sho'—sure will, Aunty."

"That's settled, then." She sighed, and was silent.

We gazed about, still marveling that we were here and safe and free in this fine place.

The main house was large, clapboard, with a wraparound veranda, blue shutters, and border gardens where now only asters and chrysanthemums and Michaelmas daisies grew. Copper beeches and wineglass elms towered high above chimneys from which smoke rose lazily like waving gray horsetails. Trees and flowers we had never known before.

There was a trim, clean atmosphere about the house, the broad lawns, the stable, the cow barn with its gilt weathercock swinging atop. There was a neatness to the white rail fences and well-hung gates. It was all so unlike the slovenly air of the plantation we'd left behind us.

I loved that Ramsey estate, in all seasons.

*　　　*　　　*

"Play me a tune, Cezanne," Tamar said peacefully. "Would you do that?"

I had just got the harmonica out when the white stable boy—his name was Bart—came from the stalls, swaggering in a way he had, and said to me, "You allowed as how you could sit a horse, dint you?"

I looked at Tamar, looked at Bart, gave the harmonica to Tamar, and stood up. "Any hoss," I said.

"That a fack? Awright. Go in there 'n' git Patrick out. Lessee you handle *him*. You know which one's Patrick? You kin read the names on the stalls?"

"Since I've been muckin' out for 'bout a week now, I kin tell which is Patrick, 'n' I kin read names good as you kin."

Faced with Bart's sneering manner, my pronunciation seemed to improve somewhat. Pride, I guess.

"If you need help in saddlin' him, give a whistle," he said with a smirk.

"Don't need no saddle."

"Wal, I'll be switched! Little darky don't need no saddle! I'll be *doggoned*."

One day Blade had said to me, "Get that there mule out to the woods 'n' hitch it to a sledge that's stuck in the brush. Damn fool mule we were usin' to haul drapped dead."

He practically tossed me on the mule's back, and I dug my heels in. After a moment of debate the old fellow agreed to amble forward. We had to cross a wide stubbly field before reaching the woods, and when I turned to look back I saw that Blade had disappeared and there was no one looking my way at all in any direction.

It was an opportunity to try something I'd often thought about.

Putting my hands squarely on the mule's broad back, I lifted my body and swung about till I faced his tail. He slogged along amiably while I did this maneuver again and again. After a while, with some misgiving, I got to my knees, first keeping my hands on his withers, then letting go. Then, with a bounce, I got myself standing. Oh, I can feel to this very day the exhilaration of clowning about on that old mule's rough, wide, wonderful back.

Afterwards, whenever I had the chance, I tried my circus tricks on mules, on large gentle horses, finally on more spirited creatures. Somehow they never seemed to mind my antics. Perhaps because I was so light? I never was much more than a featherweight.

So, on that long-ago autumn afternoon, a long way from Blade and Gloriana, I went to Patrick's stall, put his bridle on, and led him out. He was a muscular bay gelding, spirited but nice-tempered. Tamar gave me a foot up and we walked, the horse and I, in a leisurely way toward the meadow, leaped a gate, trotted awhile, broke into a canter, then galloped hard over the clovery ground, spun about, and galloped back.

Then—there was no way in the world I could resist—I spun about and rode backwards, gripping Patrick's ribs with knees that were, in those days, viselike. It seemed to me wise to wait until this horse and I knew each other better before moving on to fancier stuff, but I continued facing his tail until we were close to the barn, then spun about, brought Patrick to a stop on his hocks, and was off him, facing Bart defiantly.

"I'll be durned," he said. "That nigger can sho' 'nough keep his seat."

One second he was standing, the next he was dangling in air, gripped in Jim Maury's great paw, being instructed, in deep tones, "Take it back."

"Hey! Lemme *down*, dammit. Lemme *down!*"

"Take back that word which I deem an insult on any white man's tongue, even if the 'man' is just a trashy boy. You don't want to insult *me*, now, do you, do you?"

"No! Maury, you crazy? I don't never wanna insult you, no way at all!"

"Then say, slowly, with feeling, that you are sorry you used that word, that you will not use it again, and see that you never do use it again, or you'll be looking for work in every corner of Canada and not finding it. You hear?"

"I hear! I hear!"

"*I* haven't. Not yet."

Thrashing and kicking about, Bart yelled, "I take it back! So lemme down!"

"You haven't finished saying what I told you to say," Maury pointed out, shaking him like a dust-cloth. "Repeat after me—'I will not use that opprobrious term ever again in my life.' Say it."

"Ah gee—*Maury!* I'm stranglin' here!"

"Say it."

"I won't use that—that *what?*"

"Opprobrious term."

"Oppbo—Oppro—Oh hell, you know I can't say that. I promise I won't use no bad word to you or him. So lemme *down!*" Maury dropped him so suddenly that he sprawled on the ground, where he lay glaring at us with hatred.

Tamar and I had been watching, with relish, the confrontation between the white stable boy and the colored, now fully recovered, coachman, but I had a notion it would do me no good as time went by. Until then, Bart had merely goaded me with sneers and insults. Chances were that now he would lay all manner of nasty traps and snares when Maury wasn't around, and if I snitched on him, things would get worse.

Or—unlikely alternative—he might admit I was good with horses and let some kind of truce between us be established.

As it happened, neither one nor the other happened, because sometime in the night Bart took his gear and lit out for parts that remained forever un-known. I asked Jim if he could really fix it so a per-son wouldn't be able to find work in Canada.

"Son," he said with a subterranean chuckle, "I couldn't put a grasshopper out of a job. If any old grasshopper wanted to work, which I understand from fables they do not. Only ants."

"Den why Bart tak you so serious?"

Maury shrugged, scratched his head. "He's stu-pid? I'm so much bigger than him? Maybe because I *said* I could, and he didn't stop to ask himself how I'd go about it. Just figgered he'd better get going without a forwarding address, so my *in*fluence couldn't foller him clear across Canada." He laughed again. "Good riddance. He hadn't been here long anyway, and he kicks dogs. Besides, we don't need but one stable boy, and that one sure couldn't handle Patrick."

As Maury always had a couple of dogs trailing after him, I realized Bart's time had probably been about up anyway, so I didn't have to feel guilty. Not that I would have.

"You know many riding tricks like that?" Maury asked me.

"Sho' do. Lots. I been doin' stuff lak that since I was a real li'l fella."

Maury smiled. "That long? Well, let's you and me ride out to the far field and have some sport. I'll take Patrick and you ride Albert. Tell me, Cezanne, have you never used a saddle?"

"Not fer mysel'. I train hosses to de saddle, but only white peoples uses 'em reg'lar down dere. When I use-ta ride wit' Miss Mady, once she gib me a blanket, but I dint like it, nohow. Kept sloppin' aroun'."

"Should think you'd get mighty galled, riding bareback all the time."

"I got ober gallin' years back."

"Over," said Maury. He smiled again. "Tamar says—if you don't mind, of course—for me to continue your speech lessons."

"I doan min' atall, Mr. Maury. I aims to speak real good 'fore too long."

"I'm sure you will. And call me Maury. Or Jim. Well—let's go get them."

Maury saddled Patrick, and I led out Big Albert, a freckled, rawboned quarter horse whose head I barely came up to.

"You 'n' me's gwine—gonna do some fancy ridin', Albert. Dat suit?"

Big Albert tossed his head as if in anticipation. He was an indulgent mount who would tolerate just about any behavior in a rider. Perfect for me to show off on. Maury hoisted me up and I sat on his back higher than I'd ever been on a horse before.

"Lawdy," I exclaimed, leaning over. "Where de groun', Maury?"

"Right under his four feet," the coachman replied with a roar of laughter, and off we went.

We spent about an hour in the far field, and Big Albert performed like a circus-trained mount while I leaped and twisted and turned and stood on his back. Then, for fun, just as in the old days with Miss Mady, Maury and I galloped full tilt in a great circle before heading back.

While we walked the horses, Maury said, "You mind if I tell Mr. Ramsey about this talent of yours? I think he'd like it fine to see you go through your paces. We've never had a bareback acrobat here before. Regular centaur, you are."

"Whass a sentor?"

"A once-upon-a-time creature—Greek, I think—that had a horse's body and man sticking out of the top of him."

"No foolin'! Any a dose lef'?"

"Sorry to say, there never were any. They were a—a mythology." He added, before I could ask, "That's like a fable—something made up. Anyway, do you mind showing off your centaur imitation for Mr. and Mrs. Ramsey?"

"I doan min'. I likes showin' off."

Oh, I was proud and full of myself that day, as I walked Big Albert to cool him down, patting his high head and throwing compliments up to his ears.

Tamar, who had been packing her few things, came down from the loft just then and said that the carriage from the house she was going to, people named Harrison, had come for her.

Realizing with a rush of despair that I'd wasted my last chance to be with her, I squeezed my eyes against tears, tightened my mouth to prevent sobs.

"There now," she said, pulling me close, as she and Mam had the same way of doing. "You think I didn't like having you *play* for a while? You've never had a chance to play before in your life, Cezanne. Do you think I am not happy as can be to think you're going to be here with Jim and Mr. and Mrs. Ramsey, and that Irishwoman in the kitchen who may be almost as good a cook as my own self? Do you think all that doesn't let me go off feeling *good?*"

"But I doan feel good to hab—have you go 'way, no way atall I doan."

"Well. Go I must. And now, this minute. Good-bye for a while, dear Cezanne. You don't have to see me off, if you'd rather not."

But I walked beside her to the circular driveway, where a one-horse chaise was waiting. The driver allowed Tamar to store her cardboard suitcase inside without assisting her. I scowled at him, but as he was staring blankly ahead, my disapproval had no effect.

For the first time Tamar's resolve to be optimistic, if not cheerful, about our separation wavered. "Oh, Cezanne," she said. "What am I going to do without you? Whatever shall I *do* without you?"

Trying, in turn, to give comfort and support, as she had given it to me for so long, through so many trials, I whispered, "You cain't—can*not* be goin' far, in dat dere—that there *calash*, Aunty. I mought could *walk* to see you, far's that rig gwine go."

With a trembly smile she kissed my forehead, and climbed into the chaise. As with Mam long ago, I stood watching while someone I loved and needed was taken away from me.

But not, I told myself, turning back to the barn, not forever, and not where I don't know where, and not where I'll never see her again.

Unless I find her. Find Mam.

I had an unaltered determination to find my mother one day. I would save my wages—five dollars a month—until I had enough of a poke to get started for Texas, and then I'd go. I did not, could not, have foreseen how many years would pass before I'd be able to travel without fear of capture in the United States of America. I'd listened to Tamar's talk of war and forgotten it immediately. We had arrived in Canada in the fall of 1860. On April 12, 1861, the war between the Union and Confederate armies closed its bloody teeth on the nation to the south. It continued for four years, minus two days. On April 9, 1865, General Robert E. Lee surrendered his sword on the steps of the courthouse at Appomattox. So ended the "civil" war, at a cost never to be calculated. So ended slavery, though "freedom" for the black person, in the true, the valuable, the enfolding sense of the word, is a long time coming, and yet to arrive.

When the dust of the calash had settled, I walked slowly back to the barn and found myself alone. Maury was gone, having taken the Ramseys to town.

I sat on the bench, kicking my heels for a few minutes, then went into the barn to clean out the stalls.

Darkness gathered, and there was still no sign of Jim. Not sleepy, but very tired, I climbed to the loft. In the partition where she'd slept, Tamar's cot, stripped of bedding, seemed to me a terrible sight. I lay down on my own narrow bed, shut my eyes tight, and began to shiver, though the Ramseys provided blankets enough.

For the first time in all my life—however many years that was—I was alone, all alone. By myself. No one to talk to, to be near, to take courage from.

*   *   *

In the slave quarter, solitude was unheard of, un-thought of. In the windowless dirt-floored cabin, with its low door, its chinks that rain and wind and cold got through but somehow never the breath of spring, its smoky hearth where we cooked our corn cakes and occasional piece of salt pork, and which gave the only light we got, there had always been at least six other people besides Mam and me. When Tamar and I had run off, we'd not been separated more than a few minutes at a time. I would bathe in a stream or take care of my bodily needs with no thought of privacy, but Tamar required me to move some distance off when she was so occupied. It was the only separation we knew.

Now, with darkness filling the loft except for moonlight coming through high slatted windows, with Maury's quarters empty, I lay on my side, knees to my chest, too miserable—and in truth, too frightened—for tears. As the hours—or perhaps minutes—passed, I knew I could not stay there.

Taking a blanket, I climbed down the ladder and went along the line of horse stalls, passing up Big Albert and Patrick and a pair of carriage horses named

Raffi and Chela, till I came to where Callie, her head at the box stall window, was looking my way, as if waiting for me.

Carefully opening and closing the door, I patted her gentle face, gave her a little apple I'd been saving, asked if it was all right with her if I slept in a corner of the stall, and took her welcome for granted. Her cat, Fiddle, was there too. All the horses had pets for company. Big Albert kept a goat, Patrick roomed with one of Maury's dogs, Skip. I can't recall who (what?) bunked in with Chela and Raffi.

I pulled my blanket around me, with Fiddle cuddled in the curve of my legs, and slept—safe, companioned.

Sometime later I was sitting upright, my heart thudding in my chest so loud I could hear it.

A huge white form had sailed into the stall and landed on the wooden partition. How I sensed its presence I don't know, but the milky, macabre sight tore a scream from my throat that set the horses whinnying and brought Maury rushing down from his bed.

"Where are you?" he yelled, then located me

hunched in the furthest corner of Callie's stall, screaming and shaking. He came in and dropped to his knees beside me, and as he did the pale apparition floated away and out the door.

"What *is* it, Cezanne? What're you *doing* down—"

"*Ghosties!*" I bawled. "Dere's ghosties in dis yere place! I seen it! A big blobby white ghostie 'n' it havered ober me lak a spook! I'se *skeert* ob it, Maury! It mebbe de Holy Ghos', comin' fer t' carry me home. I doan *wan'* t' git carried home jes' yet—"

Maury put his hand gently on my mouth to stop its babbling.

"Cezanne! That was not a ghost, holy or otherwise. You saw a snowy owl, and how *lucky* you are. A beautiful big northern owl and she brings good luck to anyone who sees her."

"She do?" I quavered.

"She does. A person who sees a snowy owl is fortunate indeed, and here she came to pay a special visit to you alone! Cezanne, you have been honored beyond anything I have known before! Believe me, I would be happy as a three-legged goat with a crutch if a snowy owl paid a call on me."

*   *   *

I saw a few snowy owls after that, and they have indeed a pale bridal beauty, but I have never heard from any other source that a visit—in my case it felt like a visitation—from this great bird of the north brings good fortune to the one so honored. However, as Maury kept talking I became half convinced, so eager was I to believe him.

At length we went up to the loft together, moved my cot to his partition, and from then on I slept in a bed across from his.

It was many years after my stay with the Ramseys, after a few weeks sleeping in a Union Army stable, after the long haul to Texas and nights spent in ranch bunks, bedrolls on trail drives, miles spent on a train headed for Chicago, before I found myself alone again.

By then, it was a welcome solitude.

CHAPTER FOUR

One morning during that first Canadian winter, 1860, I woke to falling snow.

Coming down from the loft with a lantern, just after dawn, to see to the horses, I first opened the small door cut in the large stable door. It had become a habit with me to do this—to let the new day in, to survey broad acres crossed with white rail fences, gaze at tall trees, at the cow barn, the other outbuildings, at the large beautiful house. It was as if I attempted each day to paint it entire, in memory, as if I feared this landscape of liberty might fade the next night, leaving not a wrack behind.

Then my eyes would turn toward the corner room where Mrs. Ramsey slept, or didn't sleep, where lamplight always glowed behind lace curtains. Dear, loving Mrs. Ramsey. She had become my tutor after Tamar left. I'd told her of Mrs. Auld of Baltimore, who had begun and then stopped the lessons of Frederick Douglass, and how he had gone on to teach himself. I told her of the pale Maryland widow who couldn't tell black from white and had taught Tamar from the Bible until she could write as well as anyone and speak better than most.

"That was a real good t'ing fer dem to do, ladies like that," I said, mixing up my "that"s and "dem"s, but progressing, slowly progressing.

"It was heroic," said Mrs. Ramsey.

"You good too."

"You *are* good, is what you mean to say, Cezanne. But what I do carries no risk. It's just pleasure. Women like that risk the anger of their husbands and friends, the censure of society. I hear that some have actually been sent to jail. I don't think I would have such courage."

I thought she would have courage for anything, but was glad it wasn't dangerous for her—instructing a child how to read and write.

Often at night, if I had to go down to the box stalls to comfort a restless animal, I'd open the door and look toward the house, toward the light at that corner room.

One day, greatly daring, I said, "Y'all puts your light on berry—very early, Missus."

"You've noticed? Of course, you get up with the sun, don't you?"

"Beats him up," I said proudly.

"I surely don't, but my light is on all night. I'm afraid of the dark."

I stared, astonished that someone like her, *anyone* like her, should be afraid of anything. If a person was white, rich, had always been free, was also young and lovely, what could there be in the whole world to fear?

I looked, but did not ask, the question.

"Have you heard of priest holes, Cezanne?"

"No'm."

"Well—in England, long ago, there was a movement called the Reformation, which involved a great deal of hatred and destruction. Beautiful things were smashed, burned, lost forever. Churches, paintings, books. Human beings, too. Massacred, burned at the stake. Especially those who believed in the old religion. The king who started all this was a greedy brute who dissolved the monasteries in England and Ireland, which meant turning monks and priests and

153

nuns out on the highways to starve. But you see, Cezanne, there were brave people in the isles of Britain then, just as there are in the United States today. Great souls, ready to defy wicked laws and wicked rulers. And Henry the Eighth was a *very* wicked king. Charles Dickens called him a 'blob of blood and grease upon the history of England.' "

"Dat the Dickens writer you bin reading to me out of? *Pickwick Papers?*"

"That's the one, yes. Well, these people built little secret rooms in their homes, where hunted priests—nuns too, I hope—could hide until they could be smuggled out of the country." She smiled at me. "You're beginning to see what I mean, aren't you?"

"I was t'inking about dem—them—"

"Those," she corrected gently.

"Yes'm. Those. *Those* potato holes in the slave cabins that Missus Tubman 'n' her passengers hided—hid out in when de patty-rollers were atter them with de dawgs 'n' all. Dat lak—like the priest holes?"

"Yes, Cezanne," she said, bending upon me a look so partisan and sympathetic that my throat seemed to close up. "The priest holes, like the potato holes, were havens for the hunted. But they were very dark places and almost airless. To be shut *up* in one—oh, that could be, that *was* . . . ."

She shuddered, and drew her knitted shawl about her shoulders. "Anyway—one day when I was a child, even younger than you, we—my family—went to Boston to visit relatives. Massachusetts, of all the states, is the most civilized, but even there, those ghastly slave catchers sometimes entrap runaways, even free persons, and take them south in chains, back to captivity, back to . . . ."

She closed her eyes briefly, pulling the shawl even closer. "So that's how the American version of priest holes came to be. Anyway, that time I was telling you about, I was poking around where I shouldn't, being always a curious child, and got into the priest hole my uncle had had constructed. It was behind some bookshelves that were built into a door that someone had neglected to close entirely. While I was in there, and already terrified at how tiny and narrow it was, somebody did close it. I was trapped there—" She stopped and drew a deep breath. "I was in there, Cezanne, for nearly an entire morning—screaming and crying and frightened past describing—before they found me."

She smiled. "So that, Cezanne, is why you will always see my light on, no matter how early you rise. I refuse to be in the dark ever again."

That morning when I opened the door within the door to the splendor of fallen, and falling, snow—I stood motionless, staring at the blanched and silent world. In Virginia, in the winter months, there had sometimes idled down a thin fall of snow. It was never like this.

A white, undulating coverlet lay over fields and pastures, piled against fences, drifted into the farmyard, mounded gables and peaks of barns and house, rimmed bare boughs as with strips of wool, hung in swags from branches of pine and fir. The gilt weathercock atop the cow barn turned slowly in an easy wind, tossing snowy plumes aside. And softly, whitely, snow sifted in a shifting veil past that lit corner window.

"The frolic architecture of the snow," Emerson called it.

The memory takes its place beside that of the rainy night when the door to a shining parlor opened and there stood John Forrest to welcome a pair of drenched and muddy truants from tyranny, "Come in . . . thee is welcome."

Later in the morning, when sunlight turned the white drifts glossy, I took Mrs. Ramsey out in the sleigh. We sprinted through the chiming air, she bundled in furs, I in the warm sheepskin coat and boots they'd given me. Patrick trotted in his high-stepping high-class way, breath fluffing from flared nostrils, harness bells jingling. Oh, the clear frosty tone of harness bells ringing on a winter's morning! Haven't heard that in a long long time. Except in recall. In recall those bells are in my mind, as are drum taps, and the bugler boy sounding lights out, and the boom of distant cannon. In my mind, when I cannot shut it out, is the voice of the field boss, the sorrow-filled songs of field hands as they move down rows of tobacco from sunup to sunhigh to sundown, all the days of their lives. Again I hear the restless shuffle of cattle in the dark, hear an old cowboy's fiddle, accompanied by me on Cupid's harmonica, far from the barn where once he played upon it.

All, all are stored in memory along with loved, lost voices. Treasures of the past, safe from time as long as I, their keeper, am alive.

Well, back to long ago, to my first real snow.

Along the roadside, holly trees seemed marble sculptures decorated with dark green leaves and scarlet berries, and in the fields briers stood up stiffly through the enveloping white quilt, casting spiky blue shadows. It was a blizzardy winter, and Mrs. Ramsey and I often rode the same route, but it's the first joyous jingling jaunt that remains vivid in memory.

Quaker lamplight. Canadian snow. Stage sets for the drama of freedom.

In the spring of 1862, when the war in the United States had been going on for a year, Tamar left the Harrison kitchen and returned to Philadelphia to work for William Still's Vigilance Committee.

She stopped on her way, in part to visit the Ramseys, but of course, especially to see me.

Not certain what time she'd arrive on the appointed day, I finished my chores early, then sat on the bench just outside the stable, alternately reading and watching the horses race about the meadow, scatter-legged and merry in the lilac morning air.

I was reading *Nicholas Nickleby*, dumbfounded to find that white boys in England were as cruelly mistreated as black children on the plantations of America. The orphaned—or discarded—children at Dotheboys Hall were abused, despised, deprived of clothing, bedding, food, of shelter from the rage of grown-ups.

Did they know love? Of course not. They knew not tenderness, kindness, or care. At Dotheboys Hall the "pupils" were regularly caned. By a *schoolmaster!* It seemed somehow more horrifying than the brutality of plantation owners and overseers, from whom nothing better could be expected. In an awakening way, I decided that those boys were even more wretched than we, the children of slaves. Most of *us* knew the embracing, unshakable love of our parents. Even when torn from their arms, from their presence, we had had it.

My mother's love, and Tamar's, have been part of my blood, of my bone and brain, my whole life long. The children Dickens knew and wrote of had nothing to shore them up.

One day, a week or so after Mrs. Ramsey had given birth to a baby girl, I was invited to the nursery to see the occupant of a cradle that had rocked five generations of Ramseys. This one was asleep, taking no interest in a world she was now, willy-nilly, involved in.

Mrs. Ramsey gazed at her with an expression that reminded me of Mam's when she would turn her dark gaze upon my face. A universal mother-look? It would be good to believe that, though I do not. But I knew it in the quarter, and this baby, inattentive as yet, had it bent upon her as she slept in her treasured cradle.

"*Ma jolie*," Mrs. Ramsey whispered.

"Her name Marjorie?" I asked.

She put her hand on my shoulder, squeezed it a little. "No, Cezanne. It means 'my pretty, my beauty.' She is my little beauty."

"That French again?" Reading to me, she often pronounced and explained the French expressions in Dickens's books.

"Right you are."

"What *is* her name?"

"Well . . . it's Martha, after my husband's mother. But to me, she is *ma jolie*."

"Majolie," I said. "That's right purty. Pretty."

The arrival of Majolie was the reason I undertook

to read *Nicholas Nickleby* without help, Mrs. Ramsey being too busy now except for intermittent instruction. Considering the length of the book, and since I would not skip a word, it seemed I'd be a grown-up myself before reaching the end.

A shadow fell on the path in front of me and a deep beloved voice said, "To see you reading, Cezanne! All my dreams come true—to see you *reading*, all on your own!"

Leaping up, I flung my arms about Tamar, and we hugged each other, shouting and laughing, so happy that, for the moment, we forgot it was only to part again. We sat together on the bench, holding hands, words tumbling pell-mell as she sought to know everything I had done and said and thought and worn and read and laughed at and cried about and even eaten since last we'd been together, and I tried to find out everything about her world away from me.

Finally, sighing, we lapsed into a slower tempo. She inspected me closely, and said, "Some taller. But still skinny as a weed stalk. Don't they feed you properly?"

"Oh—we are well fed, *well* fed, Jim and me."

"He's your good friend?"

"Good as anyone ever—'cept you, 'cept you, 'cept you." For a moment I thought of telling her that Mrs. Ramsey was a friend too, but refrained.

"You realize it's just about a year and one half ago, Cezanne, that we first saw this place?"

"I know," I answered peacefully.

"You're happy here."

"Oh, yes. Yes, I am."

"That's good. I want only two things in life, for you to be happy, and for that war to be over."

"We gonna beat the South, you think?"

"Of course we will. How could God allow otherwise?"

Why allow wars in the first place? I thought, but did not say. For me, the ways of God continued suspect, but that was nothing to discuss with Tamar. It would send her on her way deeply troubled, to know I had doubts about the intentions of her Creator, about whom she had no doubts at all.

I said, "I been thinkin', Aunty. I think maybe I might could go down there with you. Join up."

"*No!* No, no, no! That is *out* of the question! You hear me, Cezanne?"

"Why? Other boys my age—"

"It doesn't matter that you claimed twelve years for yourself two years ago, you've only just about reached that now. And you are not—you're not *big*." She flailed about for explanations. "You are learning and growing here, getting ready to be a man. You must not *think* of leaving Canada until they've got that war over with down there."

"You said that Ezra—"

"It's nothing to do with you, what Ezra Forrest is up to. I want you to promise me, promise me *now*, that you will stay here where you're safe. And happy. You said you were happy."

"I am. Only—shouldn't I be helping, the way you'll be doing, working there in Philadelphia but still riding behind the horses? They don't make you do that up here. *Do* we still have to ride behind the horses on the streetcars in Philadelphia?"

"Yes. Mr. Still says that remains the way of it. And he says that they won't even *take* colored men in the Union Army, so there's another reason for you not to try joining up. They won't let you."

"Won't *take* us? Won't take us to fight for ourselves?"

"Mr. Still says they'll get around to it, when they're desperate enough, and he says they're already losing battles. But just now 'culluds' can only be servants in the army. You volunteer, you'll be taking care of some white officer's horses, or cleaning out the mess where they eat, carrying victuals to the troops in the field—they with guns and you without. You couldn't even beat a drum, like Ezra. Seems there's a law about it, passed way back in 1792, says colored men can't be in a white man's army. Mind, that's after we fought for independence in the Revolutionary War dying side by side with white soldiers. In fact, Cezanne, the *first* soldier to die in that war, in Massachusetts, was a black man. Crispus Attucks, his name was. Bet you didn't know that."

"No'm, I sho'—sure didn't."

"Well, now you know, and don't forget it."

"But what's the point of keeping us out *now*? Isn't the war *for* freeing us slaves? So why can't we help fight it?"

"What's the point of anything *they* do, North or South? And I'm not so sure the war is for freeing us. If they could keep the country whole—one Union indivisible, they call it—by letting slavery spread all over the place, they'd do it fast enough."

"But Aunty—"

"Cezanne, stop asking questions I can't answer, and that only make me angry. I don't want to be angry in the little time we have to be together today."

I sat in silence for a while, thinking over what she'd said. It seemed too strange to believe, that the Union Army wouldn't let black men fight for their own freedom, but Tamar wouldn't lie, and maybe after all it was not a war for our freedom, the way I'd thought.

"Then why you going to Philadelphia?" I asked. "You're safe up here too, you know. Not jes'—just me. You *said* you was gwine save up to be a teacher." Sometimes, when excited, I reverted to old speech habits.

"Never fear, Cezanne. I shall be a teacher one day."

"So why stop savin' up your wages? They gonna pay you in the Vigilance Committee?"

"No, they can't afford to do that."

"Then *why?*" I persisted.

"Because I admire Mr. Still and Missus Tubman,

and the others like them who are doing what they must do in spite of—of not getting justice. Yet."

"Will we get justice, Aunty?"

"Someday. One day, we'll be free. And maybe then get it. Or—*take* it. Take it, if we have to. Meanwhile, I intend to do what I can to help in Philadelphia. Get a job down there, earn and save there, even if I do have to ride in back of the horses."

"I doan think *I* should stay here 'n' be safe and happy if you ain't. Are not, I mean."

"Oh, Cezanne! I'm not looking for more happiness. I figure I got enough of that, knowing you, to last me for a good long time. One thing does please me *past* measure—you speak so well. Didn't I tell you you would?"

"Sometimes, if I gets excited—I mean *get*. See what I mean? Then I sort of forget. Mostly I speak pretty good."

"Jim Maury's been teaching you?"

Again I had a chance to mention Mrs. Ramsey, and again held back. I had a strong instinct that Tamar, who would approve my friendship with Jim Maury, would look without much favor upon a relationship of closeness with any white woman.

166

*　　*　　*

I leaned my head against her shoulder for a few minutes, then murmured, almost reluctantly, "Missus Ramsey says we're to eat lunch with her, in the dining *room*." Although hungry, I would have preferred to stay there with Tamar till parting time. Except then she would not get to eat either.

"Most gracious." Getting up, she knocked my book to the path, stooped to pick it up. "What's this?" she asked, frowning.

"It a book," I said nervously. "By Charles Dickens. He a—he's an English writer."

"It's a *novel!* Why are you not studying from the Bible?"

"Missus Ramsey, she teaching me out of Dickens. I like him. She read me *Pickwick Papers* first, and that was a funny book, an' now I'se—I yam—I am reading this one my ownself. She's pretty busy with Majolie. That her baby."

"She doesn't teach you from the Good Book?"

"Well, but Tamar . . . I tol' her you'd nigh about teached—taught me the whole New Testament. And we—she—decided it would be fun for me to read in other books. The Bible too. We reads—we read that,

167

too, but this here book is *fun*, with awful sad parts, too, those schoolboys in Dotheboys Hall, they treated worse'n some slave chillun—not me, I know I didn't have t'ings as bad as plenty of—"

As I saw no way to continue, I stopped talking.

We stood, I looking up to meet her loving, troubled eyes. I think we didn't notice then that I'd called her Tamar. I never did think of her as "Aunty" again.

"Well," she said. "I suppose there is nothing for me to do but accept this, too. So many changes that there is nothing to do about." She brushed her skirt down, straightened her neck scarf. "For the most part, Cezanne, you have become well spoken. I want you to know that I am proud of you. Now, shall we go to the house, as invited?"

During lunch, Mrs. Ramsey was uncharacteristically effusive, sensing, I suppose, coolness on Tamar's part, uneasiness on mine. Tamar herself was politely formal. She consented to see and exclaim properly over the baby. But we were all relieved to have the visit over. Even watching the chaise that was taking her to the railroad station go down the long road, through the gate, and away from me, perhaps for years, I was conscious of relief, and wretched because of feeling that way.

Except for Mam, Tamar was the closest to me of anyone I had ever known. But she was a person who never bent, never doubted what she believed, never admitted fear. Tamar would not have kept a lamp lit all night long because she'd been frightened as a child.

Perhaps, as a child, she was frightened, flogged, abased, abused into the strength we had recognized the day she arrived in the kitchen of Gloriana. I knew she had the scars of beatings on her back. I knew she had had her children taken from her, sold on the auction block as she was forced to watch.

She was a sword forged in a furnace that consumed some, and tempered others into steel. I, like Mrs. Ramsey, was subject to fear, and to doubt.

And still am.

Letter from Tamar, written from Philadelphia in 1862:

> Dearest Cezanne: Well, here I am, working in a hotel as a chambermaid by night,

169

spending most of the day in the offices of the Vigilance Committee, helping in the work of getting our brothers and sisters to safety. I never climb this narrow passageway, never mount these splintered stairs and walk into our small rooms that are always crowded with waiting folk, that I don't think of us two arriving here that day a couple of years ago. In the faces I see today, I see us as we were—tattered, shattered, hungry, hopeful, frightened. We of course turn no one away, even those that Mr. Still suspects of being spies, bribed with offers of money or freedom to betray us. It takes but a short while in his profoundly honest, dedicated, trusting presence to turn a would-be traitor into a disciple. Guess who came to see us the other day! Frederick Douglass! *There* is a great man. Another great man. A most imposing presence, a star for those born in shackles to steer by. He runs an Underground Railroad station in Rochester, New York, and was in Philadelphia for a visit, before going to *England!* There he will lecture on behalf of the

Union cause and against their aiding the Confederates, which they waver about doing. They haven't decided yet where their own interest lies. That interest, you understand, must come before justice, or humanity. Enough of that—it isn't news. You will be happy to learn that, like your father, Mr. D. also beat up a slave breaker. This man, Covey, was famous back then for being a first-rate breaker, able to whip the toughest, the roughest, the most unruly piece of black property into submission. Mr. Douglass, only 16 at the time, lost his temper and whipped the whipper. Covey never admitted to anyone that he'd not been able to subdue a mere boy, and even though Mr. Douglass was a slave for years afterwards, he was not flogged again. You remember I told you how he was taught his letters by the wife of his second master, a Mr. Auld, and Mrs. Auld was ordered by her husband to *desist* from the evil practice, but by then, says Mr. Douglass, it was too late to keep him in the darkness of illiteracy. From Mr. Auld's rage at the thought of a slave learning to read and write, it was made clear to him that learning was the path to freedom. What else shall I tell you? Well—I've met a young woman, Charlotte Forten, who is leaving presently for the South Carolina Sea Islands, captured by Union forces last year. The slaves there were liberated, but are badly in need of help, so isolated and neglected and misused have they been. Miss Forten is the granddaughter of a very famous abolitionist, James Forten. He was a wealthy sail-maker, a free black man who could have lived well above and away from his suffering brethren, but cast his lot—and his money—with them. Miss Forten is a dainty determined shoot off the old tree. Finally, Cezanne, I imagine you will be asking yourself—*Why doesn't she say something abt the streetcars?* I say it now. We are still not permitted to ride inside. In rain, in storm, in the heat of the day, we stand on that wooden platform behind the horses. Not just a run-of-the-mill woman like me, but adornments to the race (the human race) such as

Mr. Douglass, Sojourner Truth, Mr. Still. So now you know. Remember me, as I remember you . . . my heart spills over with love for you like a pot of honey . . .

Letter from Tamar, sent in 1863 from the Sea Islands, off the coast of South Carolina:

Dearest Cezanne: You have not heard from me in several months, and will be wondering, I know, where I am, how I am, and if you'd ever hear from me again. Always, always know that while I draw breath my thoughts will be with you, and whenever possible my pen at yr service. The reason for this gap in my correspondence is that I have left Phila (where, no, we still can't ride inside) to come here with some missionaries to teach freed negroes how to read and write—how to dress and wash and eat with seemly manners, how even to *think* for themselves. You see, my dear, these slaves—liberated by Union forces way back in '61—were more isolated by far than were we in

Virginia. They were kept so deprived of knowledge that most didn't know there *was* life beyond these islands, that there was any place in the world where black people were not in bondage, that they had a say of any kind about their own lives. They had been *freed,* and did not know it! Now, with the aid of the different freedman's societies, people like me both black and white have come carrying lamps to light their darkness. And oh, Cezanne, how they flutter at its light! How they cluster round us, reaching with their hands and minds toward the books, the learning, the promise we offer. Miss Forten, who has been here for several months, says that when she first arrived, the slaves did not understand that they were no longer the white man's property. They cringed even in her presence (she is a colored young lady, I guess I told you), and called themselves "Massa's niggers." What a difference this year has made! They are learning to read and write at an astonishing pace. They bathe, and wear clean clothes, and hold their heads high—things they were not permitted under Confederate rule. I am very happy here, finally teaching—both children and adults—although without the training I hope someday to get in a proper school. The islands are beautiful, with pearly beaches where beach plums and sea grapes and sea oats sway in the wind, and the waves come sailing into shore, all fluffed with foam. We have sunrise like harbingers (look it up) of Heaven. Peacock skies. Sunsets are sort of mango-colored, and the nights dark as those scuppernong grapes you used to love, and flooded with stars. I must go now to my morning classes, which we hold in a wooden schoolhouse built by the free men and women of these islands. And by the children, too. Everyone pitched in to make this place of learning a place of their *own*. The school is in a pecan grove, is fanned by ocean breezes, and would make a mule wish to learn. I learn something every day, from those I teach. Sundays, we hold Meeting in the schoolhouse. Miss Forten, or I, or sometimes a visiting preacher reads from the Bible and gives a short sermon. Then we sing! Oh, what glory is in the songs of souls set free! And so we help one another toward the day of true Emancipation—since, as you must know, President Lincoln's Declaration is unregarded by much of the South, and will not be acceded to until the war is finally over. And won. I hope, I trust, that it will not be too long now. I miss you, I hold you safe in my heart. Tamar.

It was not a letter I could read without recalling Mam, whose heart was pinned to mine, as mine to hers. My heart, it seemed, was pinned to several others besides. Tamar's. Mrs. Ramsey's.

I have never believed that we can love but once. I think love expands as it is given, and if you love one being, you can love many.

Probably—certainly—there are degrees of attachment and one could make lists. Should I be so inclined, of course I'd put Mam first, then Tamar, then lovely Adeline, who became my wife, and then . . .

What reason can there be for such a list?

I have loved and been loved and there is room in my heart even now for others—should they come along—to crowd in. I've always welcomed a new friend, animal or human, into my life, my affections. Into my heart.

Mr. and Mrs. Ramsey and little Majolie have a place in it where they nestle, safe as safe, always young and beautiful, upright with kindness and principle, as I knew them then. Mrs. Ramsey and I corresponded for many years, but I never saw any of them again after I left Canada.

Here is a picture painted in my memory:

Mrs. Ramsey, of a summer afternoon, is coming toward the stable, Majolie in her arms. The lady is wearing a pale yellow dress with spriggy flower embroideries on skirt and blouse, and a wide lacy hat tied beneath her chin with a white chiffon scarf. The baby—she is by now about two years old—is in a pink cotton dress, pink bonnet shading her face, white booties, and stockings protecting her from the sun's rays.

Here they come, Mrs. Ramsey smiling, Majolie happily flapping her arms since she knows that what lies ahead is a ride on Big Albert.

I lead him out, saddled, and when I'm mounted, Jim hands the little girl up. I settle her in front of me and pick up the reins.

Big Albert, who can gallop like a medieval charger when given his head, realizes that I wish a smooth ride, and off we go, he in a balanced gentle gait, Majolie crowing and bouncing for sheer joy. I've told the Ramseys many times that she is going to be a superb horsewoman one day. And so she proved to be.

Well, that's one aspect of love, a mighty pretty one.

And Jim . . .

I cared, deeply, for Jim Maury. Loved him. A companion, a teacher, a friend to me, for the four years that I knew him. I can summon at will his fine old face, hear again his deep laugh. He laughed easily. I see him in the stable, gentling a nervous colt, helping a young mare in her first delivery, smoothing the way to death for an old, weary animal. Horse, dog, cat, goat—all found the same kindness at his hands that I did.

We worked together like a well-yoked team. There

were daylong barn and stable and yard chores. There was unending attention to the horses, Jim being a good veterinarian until a "qualified" one was called on. He, of course, did most of the coaching duties, except for when I drove Mrs. Ramsey about in the pony chaise or the sleigh.

Days, Jim and I ate either in the stable or in the fields, then, come evening, in the kitchen with Mrs. Phelan serving, her back stiff, lips drawn in. Jim said that he'd long since given up explaining that he was prepared to serve himself.

"Old scorpion says nobody has any but eatin' rights in her kitchen, and some of us—that's you and me, of course—would never see the inside of the house if the Ramseys weren't invertebrates."

"Inv—what?"

"Lacking backbone. No spine."

"Mrs. Phelan knows a long word like that?"

"I endowed her with it. Give her a mite of word class." Maury liked to browse in the dictionary, besides reading his Bible. These two volumes will give a person *lots* of word class.

"Nothin' could give dat—that old *scorpion* any kind of class." I thought a minute, then said, "If Mr. and

179

Mrs. Ramsey know how she talk about them—why they keep her? Plenty other cooks around."

"Not that cook like she does."

It was true. The peevish Irishwoman was almost the cook that Mam was. Or Tamar herself.

"Does she like anybody, Jim?"

"Not that I've heard or observed."

"That's an awful way to be."

"It surely is, it surely is."

After supper each evening, Jim—teasing—offered to help Mrs. Phelan with the dishes, and when he'd been angrily turned down we'd go out to the stable, see to the horses, and then, according to the weather, go up to the loft, or walk across the fields, or just sit on the bench, talking over the world and its ways.

Often I got out Cupid's harmonica and played the same airs I'd played in the smithy years before, and on the long trek to Maryland, and to Callie that night on the paddle-wheeler, and sometimes just to myself.

Jim Maury had a bass voice, good for gospel songs. I can hear him yet, on a summer evening when the fragrance of clover was on the air and all the birds of Ontario were singing too.

Michael, haul the boat ashore,
Then you'll hear the horn they blow,
Then you'll hear the trumpet sound,
Trumpet sound the world around,
Trumpet sound for rich and poor,
Trumpet sound the Jubilee,
Trumpet sound for you and me.

The trumpet sounded for Jim in early January in the year 1865. One morning at dawn he sat up in bed and said, "Oof!" then lay down and seemed to die without noticing. I was with him. I watched him go. Our cots were so close together that I could reach across and take his near hand between both of mine, holding it hard, trying to make myself believe Jim had been called home. That's what he would have said, how he would have put it.

"Called home."

Now he would not—not ever—return to his home on earth. To Clive Court. To the Ramseys. He would never come back to me.

"Good-bye, Jim! Good-bye," I croaked. It hurt. Oh, it hurt—trying to take leave, that morning long ago, of Jim Maury, my friend.

At length I leaned over and kissed his forehead.

"You is off to the Jubilee, Jim," I sobbed. "Now you gonna hear the horn they blow! Yes, oh yes! Trumpet gonna sound and sound—when you gets there to the Jubilee . . ."

I walked slowly downstairs, trudged slowly along the winding path to the house, to tell Mr. Ramsey that Jim had gone past us.

They gave him the sort of funeral called for, in those days, when the one lost to death had been held in public esteem during life. Four black horses, great jet plumes waving on their heads, pulled a black hearse embellished with gilt swags. Their hooves were muffled in black velvet, and the horse brasses on their harness—some bearing the image of Queen Victoria, some with elaborate flower designs, others with strange, almost devilish-looking figures—gleamed like gold. The coachman and his outrider were sable figures from head to toe—black silk top hats with crepe streamers, black frock coats, shining black boots, black whip.

Patrick, riderless, walked behind the hearse, a groom of one of the guests leading him. Mr. and Mrs.

Ramsey were in the brougham, with me perched up there in some sort of mourning outfit Mrs. Ramsey had found for me. Callie, following the slow hearse, seemed, to me, to sense that the hands she was accustomed to were not holding the reins. It was my fancy, surely, but I felt she knew they would never hold them again.

There were twelve carriages in the procession, a great many for the funeral of a man who had been, after all, just a coachman. A black coachman. The explanation lay in Mr. Ramsey's glittering credentials in the country. He was not just well liked and wealthy, which might have accounted for the presence of close friends and good acquaintances, but was intimate with the Prince of Wales, who had stayed at Clive Court in 1860, on a state visit to Canada. It was known that Mr. Ramsey had declined a knighthood, which he said would be inconsistent with democratic principles. Although regarded as quixotic— for which read preposterous—such high-minded behavior, and such connections, assured that distant acquaintances, families from distant places would hurry to be part of the cortege for a black coachman.

Something, certainly, to dine out on for months.

("My dear, the affair could have been that of a recognized dignitary, and the Ramseys gave a *collation* at Clive Court, following interment! It could not have been more lavish if the corpse had *been* somebody! *And* you should have *seen* the little Ethiopian roosting like a crow up in the driver's seat of their brougham. Truly a sight to behold. A *pity* you were not invited. Oh? Out of the country at the time, were you? I see. Well, you certainly missed the obsequies of the decade . . .")

Jim was laid to rest in a cemetery reserved for colored people. Even Mr. Ramsey's influence could not have secured him a white grave, and, as both the Ramseys and I knew, he would not have wanted one. In this small graveyard, he would await the Judgment Day surrounded by his own. Our own.

When the funeral feast was over and the guests departed, heads and tongues wagging, Mr. Ramsey asked me to come into the library with him.

"Sit, sit, Cezanne," he said, motioning toward a leather chair. Green, it was, studded with nails that I had no doubt were pure gold. I sat back in it, then wriggled forward so my feet could touch the floor.

Mr. Ramsey fiddled with filling and lighting a pipe, at length fixed me with his mild blue eyes and said, "Cezanne, you are the best hand with a horse that I have ever known. But I just cannot move you up to the coachman's seat."

My mouth fell open at the words. Such a possibility had never occurred to me. "Mr. Ramsey, sir," I said. "Dat's—that's not something I had a mind to at all. Did I ack—act like I did?"

"Of course not." He blew out smoke in an exasperated way. "If you were older, or bigger, I wouldn't hesitate. But it really would look *odd* to have a boy— how old are you, did we ever settle that?"

"No, sir. I dunno. When I—when we—came here, and that was nigh on four years past, wasn't it?"

"About that, I think."

"That time I said I was twelve. But Tamar says prob'ly ten, and I cain't—can't be no way sure. Less say fifteen?"

"You don't look even that. The problem, Cezanne, is this—I don't mind being considered eccentric, which I am, but I'm reluctant to look silly, do you see?"

"Sure do."

"And to have you, in all your youth, perched atop the brougham, got up in Clive Court livery . . ."

I couldn't help smiling. "I might could be coachman on the dogcart."

Mr. Ramsey laughed, sobered, and said, "What I am getting around to is that Maury wanted you to succeed him when he retired. But of course—" He leaned forward, knocked the dottle from his pipe into the hearth, and cleared his throat. "Of course, we did not expect that to be for many years yet."

"No, sir. That we did not 'spect."

After a pause, he went on. "I shall have to get a new coachman. But I hope and trust that you will stay on, and perhaps grow up in the situation," he concluded more brightly. "What do you say to that, eh?"

I said what I had been deciding for some time, but had not got around to declaring until Jim, a man of color like me, died. "I can't stay at all, sir," I told him. "I am going down to join the Union Army."

When Mrs. Ramsey was told of my decision, she flew out to the stable and grabbed me by the shoulders.

"Cezanne! Have you lost your mind? Do you know you could be killed, or maimed, or lost, and no one would know what had become of you? Why should you do a mad thing like this, when you are safe here, and—and *loved*, and—what *can* have got *into* you?"

Her appeal, her warmth and affection, very nearly made me change my mind, but in the end, promising to write, always to keep in touch, I left the haven offered me by the Ramseys and Canada and headed back to the United States.

What Mr. Ramsey understood, and Mrs. Ramsey tried but failed to, was that since the war had finally become as much for the abolition of slavery as for keeping the Union in one piece, since Mr. Lincoln had at last conceded that there could not be the second without the first, and had therefore allowed black soldiers to enlist in the Union Army, so that there were now over a hundred black regiments (in all cases, of course, led by white officers), I felt obliged to throw my puny weight into the scales for the cause of my people.

And so I retraced the route that Tamar and I had taken four years earlier—across Lake Erie to Pennsylvania. This time, with money Mr. Ramsey had pressed upon me, I did not have to walk to my destination, which was Washington, capital of the nation, but rode the train. I had, also, a copy of *A Child's History of England,* which Mrs. Ramsey had given me, writing on the title page: "For Cezanne, who will be always cherished by—Helena Ramsey."

I have the volume still.

Perhaps I mentioned earlier that the actual Jim Crow law was not enacted until a couple of decades later, but its precursor existed then, even in the North, where by no means was everyone kindly disposed toward me and mine. Still, I was so happy to be on the train at all that having the conductor shunt me to the rear of the car seemed unimportant. Although the train was crowded with soldiers and civilians, no one took the empty seat on the bench beside me, and that didn't trouble me either. I was on my way to become a soldier myself, as eager for combat as any boy would naturally be who had read *Ivanhoe* and was, therefore, stuffed with visions of heroic deeds, dangers nobly encountered, battles chivalrously won.

When we arrived at a water stop, I got out with the others, and somewhat hesitantly approached a market woman dispensing meat patties, grog, pies, and other food and drink from a stall on the platform. She took, without hesitation or comment, my request for a patty, a small bottle of lemonade, and a gingerbread cookie, so I climbed back on board considerably heartened, and sat beside the dirt-streaked window, alternately dozing and watching the landscape jerk past.

The city of Pittsburgh presented a dismal picture of smoke-belching factories, grimy streets with rows of gray houses. It was such a wretched contrast to the fields and trees and trim houses of Canada that I turned to Dickens.

I relished his detestation of monarchs (excepting Alfred the Great) and the hatred with which he wrote about them. All that rage against those who, by accident of birth and nothing else, are rulers rather than ruled, I found bracing. Dickens, towering champion of the helpless, the homeless, the hopeless, passionately scornful of their oppressors, was my first hero writer. I read him as the train rattled on its bumpy bed. About ten o'clock the conductor turned down the overhead lamps, and we passengers fell into uneasy slumber.

Next morning the train made one of its many unexplained halts, and I stared out at a countryside that, a few years back, Tamar and I had traversed by dark, in fear and hunger. Now I was not afraid, was confident that when we reached a depot I'd be able to eat. Being the only colored person in the car, I did not expect anyone to be friendly toward me, and no one was. That didn't trouble me, but I wished Tamar were by my side so that we could speak of how things had changed for us, and how they were going to change for our people in the years to come.

Full of hope, I was, that day. Even of joy.

An English poet, Stephen Spender, wrote: *What I had not foreseen was the gradual day . . . leaking the brightness away.* I did not foresee it either. I thought the brightness of freedom for all people would grow, and glow. I thought that because the war was just, when it was over surely *goodness* would follow us, black folk and white, all the days of our lives.

Well, there you are—things worked out differently, did they not? The Bigot of Baltimore, H. L. Mencken, said all the major human problems are insoluble. Even he had to be right, once in a while.

Fields of corn shocks appeared through a low-lying mist, and there were numerous small farms by the wayside. I glimpsed an old man with a lantern trudging toward a red barn. Behind him, smoke twirled from the farmhouse chimney, so that one could picture the farmer's wife busy in her kitchen, at the start of a hard day's work. Here a mule and an ox yoked together pulled a rickety cart loaded with bricks, a weary-looking man plodding beside them. There a farmer drove his herd through a gate.

Besides these normal sights, we passed hillsides thick with the white tents of Union Army encampments. These were often so close to the rails that I could see blue-coated soldiers at their morning activities. Some stirred kettles hanging over stone-encircled fires. Others smoked, wrote letters, hung their wash from the limbs of trees, raked the grounds, split wood, sewed patches on their clothes. Two men leaned intently over a checkerboard, and another pair seemed to be having a friendly scuffle—perhaps not so friendly. One fellow stretched out on the ground, leaning on his elbow, reading a book. Many simply sat, propped against knapsacks or logs, hands behind their heads. I decided it must be a rest period before breakfast, and found it a scene so unmilitary, so in a way domestic, that had it not been for muskets everywhere in evidence, and soldiers engaged in cleaning them, these might have been men camping out, albeit in a curiously uncomfortable manner.

All at once I sat up at the sight of what had to be a small cavalry unit. In a meadow beyond some clustered tents, a troop of horses was going through maneuvers, play battles, riders charging one another, swerving before contact. I judged it to be rehearsal for the real, the bloody truth of what lay before them, and reenactment of what lay in the past.

It was when I saw those horses, and knew that many of them were sentenced to death, or to the suffering of wounds worse than death, that I understood that men, too, were not facing a drama brave with banners, with shields and lances and caparisoned steeds, as war had been in my child's mind—to say nothing of Sir Walter Scott's equally unripe fancy.

They were preparing for the scarlet pain of real-life battle.

At midmorning, we pulled into the depot in Washington, and all passengers piled out on the platform and into the city, to go their several ways.

Of my destination I was confident, except how to get there. I'd spied the cavalry unit some miles back, to the north, and planned on walking there. It was just a matter of figuring which way was north. A glance at the sun put me straight and I started off.

Washington in those days was not the gleaming, spacious city it has become, though I will not forbear to point out that it sheltered (I want another word but can't find it) then, and does to this day, the meanest of mean streets, boulevards of desperation, on the periphery of all this monumental marbling of whiteness.

The day I first saw it, many of the monuments were but half built and looked rather like ruins. The Capitol building had only part of a dome, and the White House was a modest building—rather better-looking then than now. Rain had fallen earlier. The streets were running with mud, and all manner of livestock was on the loose. Pigs rooted for garbage, of which there was no lack. Sows led their pink and squealing litters right across Pennsylvania Avenue, where hired hacks and handsome private carriages either tried to avoid them or simply ran them over and rode on. A drover led a flock of beautiful black and white and tan goats through the traffic, their bells sweetly ringing in the clamorous air. Mules with sad eyes and huge burdens were whipped along by men who seemed uniformly angry. Negro women strode with great bundles of laundry atop their heads, and I wondered whether anyone white could ever get clean were it not for the women of my race.

Mule-drawn army wagons passed, some loaded with pine coffins, others piled with what I at first thought were bodies, then realized were wounded soldiers. Perhaps in the haste of removal from the scene of battle little care was taken to arrange them comfortably, but I think cordwood would have been stacked with greater care, and I wonder still how they endured the pain of being tossed and jerked about as the wagons rumbled over cobbled streets. No doubt many succumbed before reaching a hospital, still others from the disastrous attention they found there.

With my book, harmonica, and cardboard grip containing a few clothes, and a sandwich I'd purchased at the station, I set off to leave Washington behind me as fast as possible.

The road wound uphill, and when I'd gone several miles, here came a dappled gray lickety-splitting toward me, saddled and riderless.

"Whoa! *Whoa there!*" I shouted instinctively, not actually expecting that he'd stop. But there! He slid to a skidding sitting-down stop, as if amazed at my appearance.

I approached slowly, hand of friendship outstretched, expecting he might take off when he realized that I was not empowered to give orders.

He stood. Waited for me to rub his forehead, behind his ears, run my hand down his withers. He wasn't lathered, so had not been on the loose long. I wondered where the person who'd recently been in the saddle was now.

Taking the reins, I turned him about and we plodded up the hill together, me telling him about Shenandoah.

"You might could've played together, nice as nice.

She get—got along with ever'body. Sweetest little filly you ever laid a eye on, like a spotted pup under a red wagon . . ."

He tossed his head up and down as if in agreement.

Pretty soon I spied a large, swarthy, blue-coated man shambling toward us, heavy shoulders drooping, forage cap flopping over one ear. Even his bushy mustache seemed to sag. When he saw us, he started to run, stumbling, waving his arms and shouting.

"Hey there! Hold on! That's my hoss you got there!"

When we were close enough not to shout, I saw before me a man in a sweat.

"He toss you?" I asked, politely.

For a moment I thought he'd swear at me and the horse both. Then he removed the crumpled cap, rubbed the back of his neck, and said hoarsely, "Daggone critter does it apurpose. Ran me under a branch this time. *He* coulda got someone else to— but no, it's gotta be me. Gives him a sense of power, prob'ly."

"Who?" I said, wondering if he could possibly be talking about the horse.

"The Lieutenant. Snot-nosed kid half my age. His Almightiness *Lieutenant* Farquhar, that's who." He brightened slightly. "Down with the trots today, he is. Reason he tol' me to give the daggone critter its afternoon gallop. He's usually got *some* reason why I should take the hoss out while he lays aroun' readin' manuals, aimin', y'know, to rise in the ranks. Now *I* jes' wanna get out of 'em, go back home. Today he's in his tent groanin' like a stuck pig, all fer a case a belly rumpus. Some sojer, is what I got to say. Like to see how he'll ack when he faces sumpin' *real*, like a raid, which to date he ain't."

Ignoring the lieutenant part of the story, I said, "Look—if you know the horse is gonna toss you, why don't you outthink him? Horses are right smart, but they can't outthink a good rider more'n once."

"For first, I am *not* a good rider. For second, this—this *outlaw*—never plays the same trick twice. Brute's got a *slew* a schemes to separate me 'n' the saddle, and I never know which he's sot on this time. Crowhops, you know? To make me think he's in a right good mood. Hah! Jes' when I'm fooled into thinkin' this time won't be so bad, daggone brute bucks like a range mustang. I say 'haw,' he 'gees.' I say 'gee,' he 'haws.' Balks a hedge at the last second and over I go. Fact is, the hoss plain don't like me."

"When I was on the train, I saw lots of horses up there a ways. Is that a cavalry unit you belong to?"

"Company Two of a battalion," he said gloomily. "And it's where I am *presently*. I been ever'place in this man's war, almost from the start. I'm a corporal," he said. "Permanent corporal. Made sergeant once't, but it didn't take."

"What's the horse's name?"

"Groundcover."

That made me smile. Such a good name for a horse like this, a cavalry horse, a *war*-horse. Clearly not a brute, or outlaw, except in this corporal's view.

"If you *know*," I went on, "that he's gonna pull one of his tricks, it's just a matter of figurin' which one."

"Dint I jes' finish tellin' you!" he shouted. "I *cain't* figger his bag a tricks. He's got me buffaloed seven ways from Sunday."

Suddenly I realized that I was with someone like Tamar's widow woman—a person who didn't know black from white. He was arguing on an absolutely even level of exasperation with the horse, the

Lieutenant, the cavalry, and me. With, it would seem, the entire world.

I liked him enormously.

"Can't you ask this Lieutenant whatever to let someone else exercise Groundcover?" I asked.

"Nobody can tell Lieutenant daggone Farquhar a bloody thing. 'Cepting, a course, higher officers. He's all humility aroun' them, let me tell you. But he downright loves to order the lower orders about, especially corporals twice't his age that he knows don't like him. Or hosses either, come to it."

"What are you doing in the cavalry, if you don't like horses?"

"You gonna explain army ways to me? I enlisted to fight for my principles, which is a-gin'—" He actually seemed to look at me for the first time. "Lemme tell you, son. I'm a Texan, and that state *seceded* to preteck its right to keep folks like yourself in slavery. Now, I don't no way at *all* hold with one human bein' puttin' his brand on another human bein' like some range critter. God did not *ever* intend for this to happen, and it was His mistake to let it take place in the first place, but He seen the error of His ways and got this here war going to correck it. So—being

199

a God-fearin' man of strong principles, I enlisted on the Union side to fight the evil, losin' the love of my brothers and most of my pals adoin' it. Still, God comes afore pals *or* kin. First off I was in the artillery, then I was a scout—a skirmisher—then one day when they—don't ask! they're who decide ever'thin' for ever'body else—when *they* all at once find out I'm from Texas, which I never kep' no secret, right away they think *hoss!* You'd think ever'one from Texas come outa their mama's womb on a saddle! Papa, bless him, was a vaquero from Mexico, but you'd never know it from *my* seat. My brothers can ride, right enough. But me— a cavalryman! I'm a cook, and not even good at that. Name's Trillo, by the way. Cal Trillo."

"Mine's Cezanne. Cezanne Pinto."

For the first time he seemed to relax. "Now, that's some daggone name, all right. Where'd you git a high-tone name like that?"

"I made it up, me and my mother did."

"Well, daggone. You shore did a bang-up job. Cezanne! Whatcha know. Sounds like one of them high-class Creole names from New Orleens. You got any Creole in you?"

"Not that I know. We might could be anything, you know? Not having a Bible with our family history wrote—written down in it."

"Pinto, now. Mighty like Trillo, right? Got any Mex in you?"

Again I disclaimed knowledge of ancestors further back than my parents. "What's a—a vaquero?" I asked.

"Mexican cowman. Papa was one of the top riders north a the border, and my brothers—they ain't a horse could throw a one a them." He sighed. "I jes' dint inherit the knack."

"That's a *shame*," I said sincerely.

"I'm not ashamed. If God intended me to ride good, he'd have given me the seat for it." He put out his hand and shook mine. "Glad to make your acquaintance, Cezanne. Where you bound for?"

"I thought—I had a idea I could join up with your unit that I saw from the train window. I've decided to enlist, only I don't know how. So, seeing all those horses—"

"You *like* the critters?"

I drew a breath, wondering how to put it. Finally I said, "Mr. Trillo—I mean Corporal Trillo—I think horses are the chosen creatures. I think they are the most intelligent, beautiful, loyal, the most wonderful—"

He held up an arresting hand. "You sound like my brothers that I don't expeck ever to lay eyes on again, on account of I fought on the wrong side, by their way a thinkin'. Call me Cal. So, you're sot on joinin' up, are you? Kinda young, 'cept maybe for a drummer boy."

"I'm older than I look," I said, thinking that might well be a fact. "I'm short. Always been short, but I'm maybe sixteen."

"Seein' they're after ever'body can move around without faintin', you might's well come along with me. I'll tell the loot as how you want to join up and know how to handle a hoss. I take it with all that *ad*miration you have for 'em you can handle 'em too?"

"Oh, yes," I said. "I can do that."

We continued uphill toward the camp, and as we neared it I stopped, and said to him, "Why don't you get on Groundcover and ride to the camp ahead of me?"

"Why don't *you*?" he growled.

"Your Lieutenant Farquhar might not rightly be pleased with that. But if you get on him easy like, 'n' run your hand along his withers, acting like you *like* him, 'n' lean over a little 'n' say it into his ear."

"Say what in his ear?"

"Say to him, 'Groundcover, you are one real superior hoss 'n' I find it a honor to be on your back, so you go nice 'n' easy back up to the lazy loot that's got the trots . . .' Just go on like that, and he'll know you're his friend, sure enough."

"No stuff?"

"No stuff. Try it."

He stuck out his lower lip, considering. "Done. I'll give it a try. But looky here, Cezanne—I got an idee jes' came to me, so when we get back to camp 'n' I take you to *Lieutenant* dad-blamed Farquhar, you keep mum, like you don't speak American, see?"

"Why?"

"I jes' got this notion to take that lieutenant down a peg, and yore the boy to he'p me do it. If I do like you say with this here hoss, you do like I say, that a bargain?"

I had no idea what he was talking about, but agreed to go along with whatever it was. He was such a funny nice fellow, and color-blind, except being part Mexican maybe had something to do with that.

"Get up on him easy," I said. "And remember you and him is *friends*."

He swung aboard with a thud. Groundcover put his head down, snorted, gave a couple of hoofs-off-the-ground bucks, then sprang up the road at a crazy canter leaving air enough between the corporal's bottom and the saddle that a bird could've flown through and probably back again.

Nothing I could do but look after him and laugh, before I started in pursuit.

At the brow of the hill, just outside the encampment, I couldn't at first see where my Corporal Trillo had got to, and a feeling of panic seized me at the few glances aimed my way. I was fast finding out, on this trip down from Canada, that because people were Yankees, by no means did it follow that they felt friendly toward the folk whose rights and freedom they—presumably—were fighting for. At least in part. Knowing the Forrests, Dorcas Miller, the people at the Vigilance Committee, living with the Ramseys— such acquaintance had unfitted me to be looked at this way without wanting to glare back, which at the moment I thought I better not do.

Licking lips that had gone dry, I almost turned and ran, then saw a drummer boy, white but at least younger than I so not quite as scary. I was wondering whether to ask him where I could find Corporal Trillo, when there he was himself beside me.

Drawing me a few yards away, behind a stone wall, he sat me down and spoke in a low voice.

"I'm gonna take you to the loot now, Cezanne."

"He gonna let me enlist?"

"Oh, you'll git enlisted right enough. Not by him, by the Colonel. But first—jes' keep your mouth shut, like I said, right? How'd I do on that there Groundcover, eh? Made it to camp in six minutes and one piece. Dint have no chance to sweet-talk him, mebbe I'll try that nex' time. Now, remember—you don't speak American."

"What *do* I speak?"

"French."

I gaped at him. "Why? I mean, I don't."

He studied me for a moment, rubbing the stubble on his chin. "Looky. I've took to you. Yore a nice boy and ain't no fault of yourn bein' black, but there's plenty in this here regiment might could make things rough for you, if you get my meaning."

"I get it."

"So, I got this idee, from your name, mind, that'll make things easier all around, and be a lesson for His Hossmightiness Farquhar that is jes' a jumped-up farmer that larned how to stay in a saddle, which has gave him notions above hisself. He's a snob, like most cavalrymen. Think they're God Almighty, the bunch a them, up on their high hosses—the Colonel too, he's a mite better'n the rest—'cept maybe not, it could be jes' a show he's puttin' on—"

"How can I get enlisted, if I can't talk American?"

"Plumb loco, that's what *you* are. Tryin' to git in on what most of us want to git out of."

"Why do you stay in if you want to get out?"

He gave me a narrow-eyed, almost hostile glance. "I don't *run* from nothin' that God tol' me I should take part in. Jes' because I hate this war and this company and most of these here hoss officers don't mean I'd run from *anythin'*. First the artillery with them cannons, then a turn at standin' picket. Then I was a scout, and I been in six cavalry raids in and aroun' Maryland and Virginia since bein' stuck in this

206

here hoss battalion, so *far*. On foot, a course, skir-
mishin' ahead a the troops. Let me tell you—
skirmishers takes more risks—well, jes' as many—as
those mounted raiders what jes' rush in and rush out—
but I don't run from my bounden duty, no matter
what, that clear?"

"I'm sorry, sir. I shouldn't've said that. No way
should I have said that."

"Good as forgotten. Call me Cal. Now—what I'm
sayin' is that you're the only cullud fella ever come
nigh this comp'ny, even if you ain't black as some I
seen. There's officers in other units got them contra-
bands for servants like, but none so far here, and I'm
not lookin' for you to be no servant, and I do aim to
put one over on that snot-nosed lieutenant. So, folly
me close, and lissen and don't *talk*."

"You said I'm supposed to talk French, which I
don't, but suppose this lieutenant does and he says
something to me? What'm I gonna answer?"

"He don't speak a daggone word but Ohio. A Ohio
farmer that kin ride pretty good, 'cept not a one of
'em in this here cavalry could ride ten minutes with
a Reb. *There's* natural-born horsemen, for you—good
as Texans any time. Most Texans."

"Virginians are the best horsemen in the world, I guess."

"You never said a truer thing, 'cept Texans, and them vaqueros from Mexico, like my daddy. About the Frog tongue, now. The lieutenant wouldn't know it from Chinee, but the Colonel, I dunno. Still, by the time we git to him, it won't matter. The *point* is to make a jackass outa that jackass."

I was plenty worried, but curious too, so I followed him through the tents, past soldiers rubbing saddles, shining boots, currying mounts, mucking out—chores I was accustomed to and mostly enjoyed because it was for horses.

The Lieutenant was sitting outside his tent with some other officers. Some busy polishing their tasseled swords, some smoking, talking among themselves. Corporal Trillo and I stood at a respectful distance, waiting to be noticed.

At length, one of them glanced our way, leaned over, and whispered to the Lieutenant, who looked up and said, "Yes, Corporal? Something?" His eye fell on me. "Where'd you find the little nig?"

"Sir, if I could jes' have your ear fer a moment, private-like?"

With an amused glance at the others, Lieutenant Farquhar sauntered over to us. "So, Trillo? Get on with it."

"This here, sir, is Cezanne Pinto, and he's from highborn Creole stock. New Orleens, you know, his daddy's a French prince, right over from France, and he's sent his son Cezanne here, who don't speak nothin' but Frog, up here in *indigo*—that means in disguise—"

"I know what indigo means, Corporal," the lieutenant snapped, looking at me suspiciously. "A *real* French prince, like a noble? One of those rich Creole families?"

"Right 'nough. That's him, all the way. Sir."

"So how'd you find that out, if he only talks Frog?"

"Speaks it myself, sir!" Corporal Trillo said, smiling broadly.

"Like hell you say."

Cal turned to me and said, *"Swin de perperoo ally ferdingle?"*

With an impulse to fall on the ground in a fit of

laughter, I cast about, came up with *A Tale of Two Cities*, which Mrs. Ramsey had read to me, now and then tossing in a passage of French, having me say it after her. "To give you," she explained, "the *feeling* of a beautiful tongue and a great revolution."

"*C'est Monseigneur le Marquis St. Evrémonde, Paree, Madame Defarge, le Bastille, quatorze Juillet,*" I spouted. Then, for happy measure, added, "*Jean Baptiste Pointe Du Sable,*" which Mrs. Ramsey had also taught me to pronounce.

"What in blazes is he saying?" Lieutenant Farquhar asked peevishly.

"Says he's a right smart hand with a hoss 'n' wants to *en*list in this here noble company of cavalry, sir. Serve under you, like. Says he admires your appearance." The corporal's face almost split with a smirk as he regarded the despised lieutenant's confusion.

That gentleman removed his cap, rumpled his thick hair, finally said, "Well, I'll take him to Colonel Carboy. You better come along, Corporal. To translate," he added, just about spitting the words.

"Right you are. Sir." Corporal Trillo sounded

smartly military. He probably hadn't had this much—or maybe any—fun since he'd joined up.

Colonel Carboy was at a table in a large tent with the flaps turned back, conferring with his staff. He sat erect in his field chair, smoking a fragrant cigar. Muttonchop whiskers, blue velvet coat with gold cuffs and lapels, wide-brimmed hat with a silken tassel, buttery-looking boots, sword at his side in an elegantly chased sheath, also tasseled. Fancy as a grouse in courting plumage. He had, withal, an indisputable air of command.

"Well, Lieutenant Farquhar," he said, putting aside a map he'd been studying, pointing his riding crop at me. "What's this?"

"A French prince, Colonel, sir. From a high Creole family. He's in *indigo*. That means in disguise, sir."

"Does it, now." The Colonel's lips twitched, and he fixed a keen glance on me. "Going to be traveling *indigo* all your life, aren't you, son?"

"He does not speak American, sir. Only Fro—French."

"That so? *Comment ça va, petit nègre?*"

Seeing the game was up, I glanced at Cal Trillo, shrugged, and said, "I just want to enlist, Colonel, sir. I'd like to fight for my people too, like you're doing."

Lieutenant Farquhar seemed ready to go off like a firecracker, and the look he gave Cal as good as said, "Leg irons for you from now till the turn of the century!"

The corporal retained his smirk.

"Fight for your people, eh?" the Colonel said, tapping his crop on the table. "Your people have caused a hell of a lot of trouble in this man's land, and are going to cause more. Lots, lots more."

I glanced down, lifted my eyes to meet his. "Not our fault, would you say? Sir?"

"No. God knows whose fault it is. If He knows. All *I* know is, there's been a lot of blood shed and a lot of families torn apart and a lot of—" He stopped, drew on the cigar, lifted his shoulder. "No. It's not your fault, and I *am* fighting for you, because this is the side I am on, but that doesn't mean I don't see trouble ahead. Black and white—they're never going to mix. Never."

I stood mute.

"How did you land here? In this place, I mean?"

"Saw the horses out of the train window, sir. I walked back from Washington, to join up."

"Good with horses, are you? A lot of you people are, of course."

My stomach was beginning to tighten. I'd heard downright hostility in voices that was preferable to his suavely conversational tone.

"Answer me, boy," he said, still friendly.

"Yes, sir. I am very good with them."

The avuncular Colonel gazed at his men, who looked at the ready—to indulge or despise me according to how he cued them.

"Didn't I rebuke the private who was supposed to be taking charge of Marengo?" the Colonel asked, looking up at the ridgepole.

"You did, sir," one of his aides said eagerly. "You allowed as how he'd been carelessly late in giving Marengo his oats."

"So I did, so I did. Well, then."

Colonel Carboy stood, waved the men aside, crooked his finger at me. "You have a name?"

I wanted badly to turn and walk off, but knew I wouldn't get but a few yards before I was the one in leg irons. Only generals turned their backs on colonels.

"Pinto," I said. "My name's Cezanne Pinto. Sir."

"Come along, then," he said. "I'll introduce you to Marengo. That was the name of Napoleon Bonaparte's favorite horse. Bonaparte was a Corsican general."

"I know."

"*What!*"

For the first time he sounded irritated, giving me considerable pleasure, but I replied in a suitably submissive manner, not wanting to get tossed out of camp at this stage.

"A man I knew, Colonel, sir. A gentleman name of Jim Maury who knew a lot of history. He told me. Told me Napoleon got to be emperor, but in the end got booted off—I mean, lost his throne and got sent into exile."

"Well, he did," the Colonel conceded, sounding sad. "But he was still the finest general who ever led an army. Except for Robert E. Lee, of course."

Jim had told me about Wellington and Waterloo, but I decided not to bring that up. Nor did it seem wise to ask why this colonel chose to praise General

Lee of the Confederacy over General Grant, on whose side he supposedly was.

No business of mine what generals Colonel Carboy admired.

In the stables he led me down the line of box stalls to one with *Marengo* painted on the door. At his approach there came a welcoming nicker and head tossing, the standard greeting of a horse that likes its rider.

"Ohhh, my—just look at *him,*" I breathed, lifting a hand toward his blaze, then drawing it back. "What a beauty. What a beautiful horse."

Colonel Carboy cradled the great head in the crook of one arm, his voice softening like a lover's. "He's the—the *crème de la crème de tous les chevaux du monde.* You'll know what I mean, with your French Creole background."

I swallowed. "The corporal was just—having some fun, sir."

"Oh, I know that." Opening the stall door, he said, "Saddle him. Bring him out. Fork him."

I studied the big chestnut for a moment. He seemed

even taller than Big Albert. "He maybe seventeen hands, Colonel, sir?"

"A little over," the Colonel said proudly.

That really was some bigger than any horse I'd so far known, but I would have grown a foot by sheer will power before backing down now. Going into the stall, I put his bridle on, took his saddle from the rack and, reaching as high as I could, got it on his back without blundering, got it cinched, and led him down the stalls to the yard outside.

Then I glanced questioningly at the Colonel.

"Up, up!" he said. "You say you're good. Show me."

By now a whole crowd of cavalry officers, grooms, and I don't know what all was standing about, looking on with expressions that varied from envy to interest to animosity to impartiality. Everyone waiting to see the little nig get up on the Colonel's high horse.

Well.

I kicked off the sheepskin-lined boots that Mr. Ramsey had given me and that I figured to wear till I grew out of them, then took a running jump and vaulted to the saddle. I couldn't reach the stirrups and didn't try, just touched him gently in the ribs. Off we went as if we'd been welded since birth.

Marengo and I—we came to one centaur. We didn't return to camp for half an hour. Had there been a way to steal him, I'd have never come back.

It was as if I were riding Big Albert again, with Jim beside me astride Patrick. I could feel Mam and Tamar and Shenandoah cheering me on. And William, my lost father! I wondered if he too could be somewhere watching me, proud to see how far I'd come from the slave quarter he had run from long ago.

That was in March. Three weeks later, the Civil War was over.

Cal Trillo was mustered out. I'd never been mustered in—just allowed to remain in camp because Colonel Carboy said so. I slept on a cot at the end of the stable, since the men in Cal's tent wouldn't let me in there with them. The closest I got to seeing combat was when, by accident, I encountered two cavalry officers having a fistfight behind the stables.

CHAPTER FIVE

Four years after the first Battle of Bull Run was won by Rebel troops under General Jackson, who became known as "Stonewall," after hundreds of thousands of deaths and disappearances, balance repeatedly shifting from one side to the other, opportunities not seized, battles lost through chance, generals appointed, dismissed, killed by mistake (Stonewall Jackson, returning from reconnaissance, mortally wounded by a picket who mistook him for the enemy)—after all this, on the ninth of April, in the year 1865, General Robert E. Lee surrendered, handing his sword to General Ulysses S. Grant on the steps of the courthouse in the village of Appomattox, Virginia.

The war was over, and we slaves free at last, free at last . . . unaware that the struggle to get free in truth would go on and on.

Everyone knows how, at the Appomattox encounter, Lee was courtly, Grant magnanimous.

I do not jest at scars, though I never felt a wound. Nevertheless, considering the waste and the filth and the pain, the maiming and the hatred, the dismemberment of bodies and families that led to the famous ceremony, I muse upon the "gallantry" of Lee's surrender, the "courtesy" of Grant's refusal to let his men jeer at a vanquished foe, and find it all rather preposterous.

Cal Trillo and I traveled together from the cavalry camp above Washington to a small town on the Brazos River in the south of Texas. We had a bit of money, he having saved most of his war wages, though he never did collect all that was due him, I still in possession of some of Mr. Ramsey's generous parting gift.

We took the train to Pittsburgh. Cal rode with me in the colored section, and in fact wasn't the only white man there. To begin with, the fare was cheaper, and to go on (not very far on), that was during the brief postwar period when black people, to an extent we'd never dreamed of, were fairly well treated, if not regarded. Those of us who "behaved" ourselves, that is. I behaved myself. I wanted no trouble from anyone, just wanted to get to Texas and start in looking for my mother.

"You got any notion 'bout the size of the state of Texas?" Cal asked, as the train clattered along through a landscape not pillaged and mutilated like the South.

I recalled Cupid windmilling his arms in an attempt to described the vastness into which my mother was being taken.

"It's big," I said.

"Big says it, right 'nough. Jes' how'd you propose to go *about* findin' your mama?"

"Don't know. But I'll try till I drop."

At Pittsburgh, we got ourselves jobs, for passage, aboard a steamboat going downriver on the Ohio and then the Mississippi to New Orleans.

I found it almost frightening to be going there by *choice*. The mere naming of the city—*New Orleans*—had filled plantation slaves with terror. Though now it was only to be a stopover on my way further along in a quest, the thought still made me shiver. I could not explain this to Cal, and didn't try, but wrote a letter to Clive Court, which Tamar and the Ramseys and I called "the post office," and was our means of keeping in touch.

Dear Tamar and Mrs and Mr Ramsey: It's night now, and I'm on deck, writting in a notebook that I bote in a town upriver, the light from the cabin enuf so I can write this to you, telling of how I come to be going of my own will to New Orleens that skared us so bad in the olden awful days. Now I can go into it and out of it again on a ferry to Texas and no soul white or black can stop me from my aim. It was bad to here that Mr. Linkin was assassined that way after all he did for us, but I did here that he favored sending us all back to Afrika or to S.Amerika to work the mines becase he said white and black would never mix. The kernel at the calvry camp said the same. I hope it is not true. Everbody says Texas is to big for me ever to find Mam, but I am going to keep trying till I have to giv up. I think abt all of you all the time and Majolie to she must be a real littel lady by now. My friend Cal and I work on this boat for passige hes in the boiler room stokes the furnis and I am at a sink 10 hrs a day ever day with dishes and pots. We sleep in a bunkroom with white men—Cal's white to—and one other colored fellow a cook, I tried to talk with him, but he is dum, I think. I mean cant talk, not unbrainy, as to that I dont know but a fair cook. For fun, Cal and I play domanoes, he has a old set, theres nuthin else to do. Cal cant read so I dont do it in front of him. The river is very black and only once in a while you see a towns lites on the shore. I wood not want to be the pilot of a riverboat for any money, too dangeress. I will rite again. I love all of you. Cezanne.

Many years later, Mrs. Ramsey returned this letter to me, when I told her that someday I was going to try to write a—memoir. Yes, I shall call this effort a memoir.

"Dearest Cezanne," she wrote in an enclosure.

I opened that old copy of A *Christmas Carol* the other day, as I am about to start reading it to the children for the holidays, and this enchanting piece of correspondence fell out. I don't know now why it wasn't forwarded to Tamar, but you know my habit of tucking treasures in books . . . valentines, photographs, letters, recipes, currency . . . then being quite unable to find any of it again unless by chance. I know there are other wonderful letters of yours lurking in or behind volumes in the library because I never threw any away. I *know* you wrote a few when you were on those terrible trail drives— and one day I, or my descendants, will encounter them. Meanwhile, put this in your memoirs, which by the way I should be so very happy to see if you ever wish to share them with me.

She did find one more letter, written to Clive Court from somewhere on the Chisholm Trail. I'll include it later, if I remember to.

*   *   *

"Do you know much about Texas?" I asked the black cook one day when we'd pulled up at a rickety wharf, serving a rickety Mississippi town, to off-load mail and lumber and take on passengers.

"Don't pester me," he answered. So I found out he could speak, but didn't pester him after that.

In New Orleans, the side-wheeler nosed its way through jostling river traffic to a wharf. The levee was jammed with merchants, vendors, ladies in hoop skirts, gents in top hats, people meeting passengers, getting ready to see them off. There were several lazybones lounging on bales of cotton, chewing tobacco and regarding the activity dreamily, children charging in and out of the crowds, and a lot of hard-working porters. The mate tried to make me and Cal help, *for free*, with the off-loading of baggage, claiming it was part of the bargain we'd struck in Pittsburgh.

Laughing, we ran off into the crowd. We had worked for our passage, the trip was over, we owed him nothing.

Out of curiosity, we strolled toward the town, a lacy ruin ravaged not only by Federal troops but by its own citizens, who, during the final days of the war, in a frenzy of hatred and despair, had almost burned it down so as to keep anything of value from falling into Yankee hands.

There were some shops open. In one Cal purchased a lace-trimmed pink hat for his mother.

"What I'm hopin'," he explained, "is that the brothers will be away, so I can jes' duck in, pay my respecks to Mama, give her this here bonnet, and head on out afore they know anythin' about it."

"Suppose they're there? What then?"

He shrugged. "It'll be not so nice's t'other way, but we'll still go on in. I got a right to see my own mama, give her a bonnet, after all these years. Those fellas wanna cause trouble, I kin give it them. Easy. You he'p."

"How many are there?"

"Jes' two."

"They as big as you?"

"Warn't when I left, but they might've growed some."

"Well, I'll help all I can."

At a bookstore I bought a dictionary, a grammar, and a copy of *Oliver Twist*, as I'd read *A Child's His-*

tory of England to tatters. I needed the grammar and dictionary because I wanted to learn to speak and write correctly, so as to be a credit to my teachers—Tamar and Mrs. Ramsey. The novel, I got because it was cheap (secondhand) and by Charles Dickens. At Clive Court, under the tutelage of Mrs. Ramsey, I had become a Dickens lover and remain one to this day. There are those who apply to him words like "sentimental," "verbose," "melodramatic," other such adjectives. I say that, of all writers, Dickens was the most passionate with pity. Of all writers, he spoke for people who couldn't then, cannot now, perhaps never will be able to speak for themselves.

Besides, he wrote good books.

I was unaware at the time that I'd chosen a novel with the last forty pages missing. I shan't forget the shock of that discovery.

We took a steamboat to Galveston, then the overland stage, aiming for the Brazos River, near which Cal's family's spread was.

Or had been.

Everywhere we went I expected to be refused passage, but never was, perhaps because Cal, with his heavy shoulders, great bristling mustache, and moody eyes, looked pretty ferocious as he said softly, "He's with me."

Texas alone, of Southern states, experienced no Union incursions, knew nothing to approach the savagery that the rest of the South endured during four years of fraternal hostility and hatred. The state was not visited by William Tecumseh Sherman, a general so successfully brutal that he was honored in a later war by having an armored tank named for him, and *there's* glory for you!

After we'd got out of the piney woods and grasslands of the coastal plains, it became evident that the tentacles of war—poverty and neglect—had nevertheless managed to reach Texas, too. The stage bucked like a pony along rough plank roads and rutted trails, across flat, arid, treeless plains, past abandoned ranches, fallen fences, windmills with broken arms. Besides these symbols of desperation, there was only tableland and scrub for miles and miles in all directions. Dust rose behind us, swept toward us in the hot, dry winds. Dust got into the coach, into our clothes, our hair, our nostrils. After a while conversation ceased because no one wanted to open his mouth.

We rattled along in that manner for two days and nights, stopping twice at crossroads where passengers could get a gristly meal and a dirty bunk for the night. We managed to eat, but slept outdoors on the ground, our knapsacks for pillows.

On the third afternoon, somewhere in nowhere, Cal knocked on the roof of the stage, and shouted to the driver that this was where we got off. Taking the knapsacks, in which we had our extra socks and underwear, I my books and mouth organ, Cal the bonnet for his mother and his battered set of dominoes, we pulled our bandannas over our noses and watched as the stagecoach lurched into the shimmering distance.

In Galveston we had bought, with almost the last of our welcome Union money—Confederate currency was worthless—a couple of tin canteens, wide-brimmed hats for protection against the sun, and several bandannas each. I can't think how many of those big red and blue cotton handkerchiefs I wore out on trail drives during the next few years, when the cattle and the wind raised so much dust that even to see where to sling a rope was sometimes impossible, when it was so hot that the sun burned the back of my neck, or so cold that I'd wrap a handkerchief over my ears and under my hat. On the trail we used them for washcloths, or for tourniquets if someone got bitten by a snake or was cut and bleeding.

And you could blindfold a nervous pony with a bandanna. What they don't see doesn't frighten horses, which makes them the opposite of lots of people, me included.

That day I had no notion of becoming a cowboy. I had no notion of anything except that I was thirsty, and we'd emptied both canteens.

"Cal," I said. "Where are we?"

"Wal. That's a question, ain't it?"

"Wal," I echoed irritably. "I put it, dint I?"

He cleared his throat. "Somewhere hereabouts is my mama's ranch house and bit of a spread, the BoxK we called it."

"Where your brothers are."

"Mebbe. Cain't be sure till we get there."

"Where's *there* at? I'm awful thirsty."

"Now, now, Cezzy. Don't fume." Cal studied the sky a moment, turned right, and said, "Hafta walk a piece. In answer to your question, we should be somewheres near the Brazos. Leastways, if my calcalations is on target."

I didn't ask what if his calculations were way off. The sky was high, cloudless, white with sunlight. The only growth was mesquite and chaparral, the only life a pack of peccaries that ran across a ridge, a jackrabbit fleeing an enemy we didn't see, and a few buzzards lazing above in confident circles. Far across the plains were red sandstone buttes in strange, magnificent formations that I did not, that day, appreciate.

We walked for hours with nothing to either eat or drink, and at dusk arrived at Cal's mother's ranch and the little spread, the extent of which was difficult to estimate, since the land simply stretched off to the horizon, and I could see no other dwelling.

There was a barn with a large paddock next to it, in which a gray mule and a cow with calf lifted their heads and watched us briefly. The low, fairly large wooden house had a three-quarter wraparound porch on which were five rattan rockers. One window was broken and protected with board. In the unfenced yard some chickens pecked about. There was an air not so much of neglect as of someone trying hard to keep up, and falling steadily back.

A large red hound got to his feet at our approach, then moved toward Cal with a tentative wag of the tail.

"Beggar?" said Cal, going down on one knee. "That really you, old sport?"

With a yelp, the dog flung himself at the man, who hugged and pounded him enthusiastically. Over the animal's head, he looked at me and said, "It's Beggar. My old hound dawg. Daggone, he must be fifteen years old, an' I been gone five of 'em, an' he still remembers me. Wal, old Beggar, you old son-of-a-gun."

It was a joyful scene that I could not fully appreciate, my eyes fixed upon a well with a bucket perched on the rim. I glanced at Cal, now standing with one hand on the dog's head as he regarded the house expressionlessly.

"Cal," I said hoarsely. "Could I—could we have a drink from that there well?"

"Huh? Oh, sure, sure, Cezzy. He'p yoursel'."

He licked his lips, dry and cracked as my own, and walked slowly forward, up the front steps, through the half-open door. Beggar followed him as far as the porch, then stood, still wagging his happy tail.

I had drawn up a bucket of wonderful, blessed water, had drunk about six times from a tin cup chained to the rim, had poured another bucketful over my head before Cal came out of the house and across the yard.

"Nobody in there," he said, when he'd drunk his fill.

"Maybe they're—maybe she's—" I turned all around, still seeing nothing but this house and yard, and miles of what Cal said was buffalo grass, good forage. "Where do you suppose somebody is?" I asked clumsily.

He pushed his hat back, scratched his brow, sighed heavily.

"Someone's livin' here, awright. There's a pantry with supplies. Only but one room with a bed looks like someone's sleepin' in it. Beggar here and the other critters look like they're eatin'. Guess we'll jes' hafta settle down, wait to see what turns up. Who turns up."

He started around to the back, with Beggar and me following.

Having spent my life in Virginia and Canada, I was accustomed to what I considered real trees. Oaks and maples, beeches and birches, Norfolk pines, elms, hickories. I'd not seen anything I considered a proper tree since we'd reached Texas, except for those pines near the coast, and they weren't much.

But this country was rough—thick with brush, cactus, and all sorts of scrubby growth.

"What're *those* called?" I asked Cal, indicating a stand of stumpy trees with what looked like pea pods hanging from their branches.

"Mesquite. Pesky things," Cal said absently. He was staring at a little fenced plot on a low knoll, beyond which was a stand of deserted beehives. "Cezzy—looky there. What's inside that there fence? Go see for me, will ya?"

I walked slowly toward what by now we both knew

was a grave, kneeled to read words burned on the wooden marker.

Madeline Lucy Trillo. 1809–1865. Forever remembered.

There was an angel burned above the words. I could draw that angel today, and still think it a work of high and awkward and loving art.

I got up, turned to find Cal standing beside me, hat in hand. We stayed there, not speaking, for several minutes. Then Cal went back to where we'd dropped our knapsacks, returned with the lace-trimmed pink bonnet. He leaned across the fence and carefully placed the hat on top of the marker.

"Wanna leave me alone fer a spell, Cezzy?" he said.

"Sure. Of course."

I didn't say—couldn't say—that I was just about crazy for something to eat. I left him there with his hound dog, walked back to the yard where the well was, and drank more water in an effort to fill my belly. Then I sat on the ground and tried to study in the grammar book. I couldn't very well go in the house and find the pantry where supplies were and help myself, though I was reaching a point of nerving myself to do so.

In time Cal came back and sat beside me, twirling his hat, tossing it up, catching it.

"She'd've liked you, Cezzy."

"I figured you got your color blindness from someone."

"Yeah. She plain liked anyone nice. White, black, Mex, Red Indian, dint make no matter to her, iffen a person was jes' nice."

"She sounds lovely." He hadn't mentioned his father, and I didn't see that it was my place to inquire.

"That board there—it gives her dates, don't it?" he asked.

"Yes."

"When did she—what year did she pass?"

"This year, Cal."

"Can you figger how old she was?"

After a moment, I said, "Fifty-six, I think."

"I see. Not so old. Not young. But she had a hard hard life, and it dint he'p none, havin' me 'n' the brothers takin' sides a-gin' each other."

"You didn't take sides against *each other*, Cal, did

236

you? You fought for what you believed in. I guess they did too."

"Funny, how God tol' me one thing and tol' them t'other. That's sumpin' I cain't work out for myself, nohow."

Maybe God couldn't make up His mind either, I thought but was wise enough not to say. With Cal, as with Tamar, you did not question the Creator's mysterious ways, or express doubts as to how He went about performing His wonders.

"Still came out to Mama in tears," Cal was going on. "Ah, blast and daggone it." He beat the ground with his fist, then smiled a little as Beggar licked his ear. "Wish I could've wrote to her. I should've ast you to write a letter for me."

"I would've been glad to."

"Yeah. Wal, I dint think." He leaned forward, put his head in his hands, and stopped speaking.

Wondering just how crude it would be to inquire about food, I looked around desperately, then scrambled to my feet at the approach of a rider on a buckskin horse that looked to me as if he had more years behind him than ahead. The horse, that is.

The rider resembled Cal. Same exuberant mustache, same high cheekbones and dark eyes. He held the reins in his left hand. The sleeve of his right arm was pinned back, empty.

"Cal," I said. "Somebody's coming."

Cal looked up, jumped to his feet, started forward, stopped and stared. "It's my brother Jacob. God, Cezzy—he's lost a arm!"

The man rode up to the barn, slid out of the saddle neat as could be, stood a moment with his mouth screwed up, looking from one of us to the other, then turned and tugged at the leather strings holding his saddlebag, dropped it to the ground, reached under the horse, undid the cinch, pulled the saddle and blanket off and slung them over the paddock fence.

With an air that forbade offers of help, he went to the well, let the bucket down, hauled it up, toted it over and set it on the ground for the horse to drink. Then he took a gunnysack from a hook on the barn wall and started rubbing the animal down.

All this without a sound, while we stood watching.

*   *   *

238

At length, Cal cleared his throat. "Reckon y'all mean, by this heah silence, Jacob, that me 'n' my friend kin make tracks? Got that right, have I?"

Jacob Trillo shoved his sombrero back, lifted his shoulders, shook his head. "Might's well come on in, when I'm through here," he said in a raspy voice. He finished rubbing his horse down, patted him on the withers, said something to him that we couldn't hear, and led him into the barn. Coming back, he leaned to pick up the saddlebag. I moved forward with the idea of helping, but stopped at his expression.

He went up the porch and into the house ahead of us, and I said, "Looky here, Cal, you go 'long with him. I guess I'm the one better make tracks."

"Like heck you do that. This here's Mama's house, and she'd have welcomed you."

Too late for that now, I thought, dithering on the doorsill. I did not want to stay, I did not want to go. I thought that if brother Jacob would just give me some bread and a bit of meat, I'd go eat in the barn, sleep the night, and leave next day.

But Cal grabbed me by the shoulder and pulled me along with him into a house that was sparsely furnished, with most surfaces dusty. A few touches of Mama were there in the form of tatting—antimacassars, a table runner. There was a framed sampler on the wall. Under it, on a table, was a studio photograph of a man in full vaquero regalia—white hat with snakeskin band, black leather vest, fringed *chaparreras*, *reata* in his hand, dress spurs with jingle-bobs and heel chains on a pair of what had to be just about the fanciest boots any cowboy ever wore. There he stood, in front of a painted backdrop of clouds and cactus, looking very like Cal and his brother.

"That your daddy?" I whispered.

"Shore is. Taken in San Antone by a fellow calls hisself a dagarotypist," Cal said proudly. "That there's Jorge Pasquale Trillo, father of me and my two brothers, Jacob and Carter. Daddy passed a long time ago, kilt in a shoot-out he had nothin' to do with— was jes' on his way 'crost the street to the barber to git a shave when these bandidos come roarin' down the street and one a their bullets caught him right between the eyes. Like to broke Mama's heart. If he hadda shaved hisself, he'd mebbe be alive still, but he shore liked cosseting." Cal turned to his brother.

"Where is Carter, Jacob? How come you don't say a word 'bout Carter?"

"Don't rightly know," Jacob said. He put a kettle of water on the iron kitchen range. "Coffee in a few minutes. Y'all want somethin' to eat? I got jerky, hardtack, molasses, some honey left over. Bees is gone."

Cal glanced out the window toward the fenced grave plot. "When did Mama pass?"

"Round six months ago."

"It was you made that marker out there."

"Yup."

"It's a good piece a work. That angel. Very nice, Jacob."

"She forgive you, Cal. Said fer me to say so if ever I laid eyes on you a-gin, 'n' here you are, so you'll want to know that Mama did forgive you."

"Fer what?"

"Dint say. Jes' sent her forgiveness. I reckon it was fer goin' to fight alongside the enemy."

"Depends on who you think was the enemy, don't it?"

"Past 'n' done with. I got no quarrel with you. You

dint personally wreck the South 'n' bring it to ruin. Jes' he'ped."

"I took the path God pointed out fer me to take."

"Wal, God done tol' me the plumb opposite. Texas should never a joined either side, is what I say. But— there it is. Over 'n' done with. South's a shambles, and *nobody* won. 'Cept—" He indicated me with his thumb. "Who is he?"

"This's my friend, Cezanne Pinto. From the cavalry unit I was last hitched up with."

"Cavalry? Kin you ride?" Jacob asked, looking at me directly for the first time. "Kinda small, ain'cha?"

"Lemme tell you, Jake, this's the daggonest buckaroo on a hoss you ever *be*held."

"Kin you rope?" Jacob asked, ignoring his brother.

"No. I never tried."

"He could shore 'nough larn. He's a right smart young'un. Reads, writes, uses good long words. Smart, that's Cezzy."

By now my eyes were glazed from hunger, and Jacob all at once seemed aware of it. He got up, plunked a piece of beef jerky, some hardtack biscuits, a jug of molasses, and a jar of dark honey on the table, then poured three large cups of strong black coffee.

"He'p yourself," he said. "You too, Cal."

Cal and I helped ourselves. Liberally, frantically. It was half an hour before I was in shape even to say, "Mr. Trillo, I thank you for the food because I just did need it very bad, and I think I'd better be on my way now—"

"Hold on there!" said Cal. "You're agoin', I'm agoin'. Leastways I know *who* my friend is around heah."

"You hear me say anythin' 'bout anyone makin' tracks?" Jacob asked. "You're the one said that, not me."

"Wal, let me tell you right out, Jake. I do *not* git a feelin' of bein' well and warmly welcomed, if you git my drift."

"I git it. I ain't use't to talkin'. Mama was in a coma like, couldn't say a word for a long spell 'fore she passed. And Carter . . . Carter never come back from the war. Don't know at *all* what happened to Carter, 'cept he never come back. I come back, minus a real important part of me as you been nice 'nough to make no comment on."

Cal screwed up his face. "Dint know should I make mention or not. It's a daggone shame, Jake. A heck of a daggone shame, and I'm real real sorry. 'Bout Carter too. I'm sorry 'bout him and what mighta happened to him, which mebbe he'll still come back one day."

"Yeah," Jacob said. He heaved a great sigh. "Hosses ran off when I didn't have no more feed 'n' they could find plenty a grazin' out on the range. Only Chuck stayed with me. I figger he figgers he's too old to stand up to them wild mustangs."

"That there mule in the paddock—would he be old Amos, still friskin' among us?" Cal inquired.

"It's Amos right 'nough. Not much frisk left in the old feller. I jus' keep him fer Mama's sake, she favored him so. He kin do easy jobs 'n' is real friendly like, fer a mule. Don't even eat much."

"Things is bad, ain't they," Cal said, not as a question.

"Mebbe could get worse. Don't rightly see how."

"You want Cezzy and me to stay aroun', he'p get you on your feet a-gin?"

Jacob, putting his one hand behind his neck and

squeezing hard, said with his eyes closed, "I'd welcome that."

At that time, millions of Longhorns and mustangs
roamed at will across the endless prairies of Texas.
There were no fences, and cattlemen, before the war,
had relied on brands to mark what they called their
"critters," or simply "cows," meaning any cattle. Before the war, there had been some roundups and trail
drives, mostly up the Western Trail, but with so many
men away fighting, most animals simply went off and
lived wild. They were tough and fast and wily. Hiding in brush and chaparral thickets by day, they foraged at night, spooked easily, but also attacked sometimes. It took expert ropers and riders and bronc
busters to bring the mustangs to heel, make good cow
ponies out of them. Then they'd go after the
Longhorns, round them up, brand them, start them
on the drives north, where they brought a good price.
Because they were so plentiful, cattle in Texas were
of almost no value, but northern, eastern, and far
western states were beef-hungry and paid good cash.

*   *   *

"Trouble is," Jacob said next morning after breakfast, as we sat on the porch drinking coffee, "that even with them critters free for the takin', I can't rightly go out after the cows *or* the broncs with only one arm. Still can rope anythin' runnin', but cain't grab holt of the pommel. Makes me leery a fallin' off, mebbe breakin' a leg or this here leftover arm. Out there on the prairie, might be nothin' but a buzzard or some ol' dog coyote ever find me."

"So—how you bin makin' out?" Cal asked.

"I kin do fer myself well enough, round the place here. That there cow calved a few days ago, 'n' that'll keep me—us—fer a spell. Chickens are still alayin'. There's feed fer them in my saddlebag. The well ain't gone dry. All in all, I bin makin' out. But it would shore be a downright blessin' if Cezzy here could learn to throw a rope, then him 'n' me could go up to Ewen Frost's RollingQ ranch and offer to throw in with his roundup. There must be a few hundred critters with our brand on 'em roamin' around out there." He turned to me. "Our brand is the BoxK, for when we had a ranch to go with it. We could join up with the RollingQ when they start north, mix our critters with

246

Ewen's. He says he'd be glad to let me do that, but I couldn't expect him to do my roundin' up, too, now could I?"

"No," said Cal. "That'd be out of the question."

"What the Sam Hill was *you* doin' in a cavalry outfit, Cal? You larned which end a the hoss to face?"

"Nope. Don't like 'em one bit better'n I ever did, no matter which end I'm starin' at. *They* jes' plunked me in there. I cooked."

"Do that any better'n you used to?" Jacob asked, smiling for the first time since we'd met.

"Naw. Reckon I'm not much good fer much. But willin', downright willin'. But lemme tell you, Jake . . . Cezzy here will pick up the hang of ropin' in no time. Won't you, Cezzy?"

"Well, maybe—"

"In no time *atall*."

Jacob sat a while longer in silence, then glanced at my feet, still in the Canadian sheepskin-lined boots. Mighty uncomfortable they were in this part of the country at this time of year.

"Come on along," he said, crooking his finger at me. "We'll git you a pair a boots. Cain't ride or rope without wearin' proper footgear."

Trailed by Cal, Beggar, and me, he went out to the barn, to a corner where a large, badly cracked leather trunk, knitted over with spiderwebs, stood in shadow. Brushing aside the spider's labor, Jacob dragged the trunk to the middle of the floor, where the sun from the open door reached it, threw the lid back and disclosed what had to be the world's largest private collection of outworn shoe leather.

"Son-of-a-gun," Cal whispered. "That mus' be ever' daggone pair any of us ever stuck in a stirrup."

"It was Mama," Jacob said. "She'd come out here 'n' jes' sorta sort through 'em. Yourn, mine, Carter's. She'd set 'n' hold one a Papa's to her face 'n' plain cry. I tried hard to git her to give 'em up, but she wasn't havin' none of it. Said Papa's soul was in his boots."

The two brothers reached in and started removing footgear, laying it out on the worn board floor.

"These were Papa's," Jacob told me, lining up three sets of hand-tooled boots. One pair I recognized as those in the photograph. The finest, fanciest foot-

248

wear I ever did see, including anything worn by those dandies the cavalry officers of the Union Army, were the boots of Jorge Pasquale Trillo, a man who liked to cosset himself. Blue and gold and red designs— flowers, stars, a moon on each one—were etched into fawn-colored leather that was still supple and clean. When did he wear them that they should look so new? I wondered. For parades? Celebrations? Possibly just that once, to be photographed in, before a bandido's bullet cut him down on his way to be shaved?

Fact is, I plain fell in love with those boots, and Cal and Jacob knew it. Years later, for a gift, they sent them to me, spurs with jinglebobs and heel chains included. I still have them, tucked and tidied away. Don't get them out often, but I know where to find them.

"Only three pair?" I said that day. "Was he very young when he got—got shot?"

"Papa'd wear a pair a boots fer years, takin' care a them like they was alive," Jacob said. "Had 'em all made, by hand, in San Antone. So did we, right, Cal? Nothin' but hand*made* for us Trillos, in those days. No, not so young. Lived to be somewheres in his forties. He was cattle boss on a Mexican ranch for years. Made enough to come up here in '41—that was when Texas was a republic by its own self. Proud days. Anyways, Papa bought this spread 'n' raised stock. Had some good hands on the place, dozen or more good hosses, coupla thousan' head a cows 'n' beef cattle. All the critters ran off when the daggone war came. Mama tried to keep the place goin', but first Carter took off to fight, then—"

He glanced at Cal, now seemingly without bitterness. The two of them had sat up late after I'd gone to bed in one of the bunk rooms that had been used, before the war, by cowhands. The only two left of a family that had once been close, they'd found, I supposed, a place of understanding again.

I thought of my own mother, who so loved my father, William, who had run off because he could not do otherwise. I thought of how close she and I had been, how I had told myself, from the day Tamar and I became runaways, that one day I would come to Texas to find her. My dream, all these years, had been that sometime and somewhere Mam and I would be together again.

Only now did I begin to wonder if Cupid and Tamar

and Cal had all been right when they said there was no way for me to find her, that Texas was too big for the dreams of small, unimportant beings.

I was beginning to believe them, but not ready yet to give up.

Listening to the history of the boots, I learned how their mother had put each pair away as her boys outgrew them, how she'd put their adult boots in the trunk "for safekeeping, for when you come home," as they'd left, one after the other, for the war. How, finally, she laid her husband's three pair on top of the others and closed the trunk for good.

When Jacob came back with his empty sleeve, she told him about the trunk, but hadn't looked in it again. He only opened it long enough to get an old pair out for himself.

It seems sort of quirky—saving boots that way. But, for me, there is something touching in the sight of shoes molded into shape by someone whose step you will not hear again.

Cal and Jacob found a pair of Carter's cowboy footwear, worn when he was in his teens, that fit me remarkably well. They had pointed toes, for easy sliding into the stirrups, high heels to give a good hold on them. I tugged them on by the mule ears—loops at the sides, to help a man get the dang things on—and strode about manfully, filled with pride.

A few weeks later, wearing Carter's boots, Carter's fringed chaps, astride Carter's saddle, carrying Carter's lariat, I followed Jacob and Chuck to the RollingQ ranch. I was on Amos. We'd left Cal behind, happily painting and repairing.

Ewen Frost was preparing for spring roundup, when he and his men would be joined by crews from two other large spreads. About three hundred cowboys would begin scouring over a hundred square miles, sweeping the plains, searching mesquite and chaparral thickets, dry washes and gullies, in search of far-roaming Longhorns that had foraged on the lone prairie all winter and were of no mind to obey men or horses. This was the way of the roundups—stubborn men, who always won, driving obstinate animals that always lost.

Modern cattle—fatlings penned, nurtured, vitamin-stuffed—make better eating than the herds of the open range did. But only the Longhorn—speedy, sinewy, immensely powerful, backed by an untamed ancestry that had shaped him to withstand drought, heat, blizzards, hunger, thirst, taught him to paw through deep snow for blades of grass and subsist on those—only *he* could have survived the great trail drives. The Longhorn was wily, he was tough, and he was noble. In his contest with the cowboy, over two or three decades of trail-driving, he was always the loser. He lost, at length, his fight to exist.

In legend, he is imperishable.

Each morning of a roundup saw fresh herds driven toward a central point, then kept from escape by cowboys riding around and around, forming them into a tremendous wheel. Bellowing cattle, whistling, whooping cowboys, snorting ponies—all of them milling about in cyclones of dust—created a hullabaloo like no other on earth.

After a quick lunch, each outfit spent afternoons sorting out cattle by brand. Calves dropped during the winter would stay close to their mothers, and they'd be caught and branded on the spot. Every ranch wound up branding some mavericks, plus motherless calves.

*   *   *

I hated the branding.

Having written those four words, I've sat a long time trying to find a way to justify working where cruelty was part of life. A never questioned part. I say I was young, I was heedless, I had seen much cruelty already. I say I let myself believe it when cattlemen claimed the animals didn't suffer. I say I wanted so much to be a cowboy. None of that is justification, because there isn't any. I did it. I took part. I am ashamed.

A roundup was a huge operation, involving many wagons, riders and ropers organized into squads, with a remuda for each squad. A remuda? No reason you should know. A remuda was a string of cow ponies, usually ten to a man, that the wrangler had charge of, letting them out to graze at night, bringing them in, at dawn, to a big rope corral close to the chuck wagon. After a breakfast of pancakes, biscuits, bacon, coffee, the riders would go to the corral and rope their morning horses. These cow horses—most of them former plains mustangs—had great stamina, but not the stamina of men. Horses worked only three or four hours a day, and not every day at that. A cowboy might shift his saddle from morning horse to afternoon horse, even sometimes to night horse, depending on the size and temperament of the herd, and the number of incidents—like stampedes, storms, floods. He could be in his saddle sixteen straight hours, with a snatched moment for grub and a smoke. On a savvy cow pony, he could sleep in the saddle, relying on his mount to let him know if an animal had decided to opt out of the herd and seek its fortune elsewhere. Few of these truants escaped recapture.

And the roundup was just the beginning. When it was finished, and the cattle destined for market were herded together, Longhorns and men would start up the trail to Kansas, to Nebraska and South Dakota, even—on the famous Goodnight-Loving Trail—to Wyoming and Montana. A drive could last for months, at the end of which most hands collected their pay and rode into town to get barbered, bathed, to meet the dance hall girls, often to get drunk, cleaned out of their wages, sometimes tossed in jail. Then, until they reached middle age—twenty-five or -six—and so were too old for the life, they'd head on back to Texas to start all over again.

The cowboy of the drives is, I grant, a fellow of romance. I wouldn't mess with a myth, but will say that we cowboys ourselves (and we *were* mostly boys— maybe a trail boss would be close to thirty) didn't know beans about the glamorous life we were leading. Not, that is, until the days of the great cattle drives were over and we could safely reminisce, and exaggerate, and lie, and now and then tell the truth.

As time passed, as those larger-than-life *Riders of the Purple Sage* and the smiling *Virginian* came galloping into the picture, as the movies established their tinselly misrepresentation of a life that had been absolutely real, the history of the western prairies got duked up past recognition, and paled to unblemished white. The truth is that there were thousands of black faces under those sombreros, and plenty of us black fellows were top hands. A few—a very few—became trail bosses. And, for the most part, black and white mixed together with little fuss. I'd say cowboying was as unprejudiced a trade as any ever pursued in these United States of America, but that easy mingling came to an end when the Longhorn passed into history.

*   *   *

That day, when Jacob and I rode up to Ewen Frost of the RollingQ, he sized me up, and said, "Can he ride something feistier than that old mule of yours, Jacob?"

"Bring out any beast you like, Ewen. You'll get the surprise a your life."

Frost signaled to one of his men. "Bring out that pinto Charlie says is half broke. Got a squirt here gonna fork him. If he can."

A *pinto*, I said to myself, with a deep satisfied breath. Shenandoah, stand by me!

A cowboy that I got to know later on, name of Pete Wilson, led a bucking pony across the corral, shoved him up against the fence, looked a question at Mr. Ewen, who looked at me and said, "There he is, son. All yours."

I walked over, carrying Carter's saddle, and put it on the fence a few yards down from the horse.

"What's his name?" I asked.

"Ain't got one. Charlie, the bronc buster, jes' turned him over to us, 'long with a bunch of other half-broke young'uns."

"All right if I call him Shandy?"

"Call him anythin'. Iffen Mr. Frost decides to use

him, he'll decide what to name him. You got a passel a onlookers, so git to it."

Glancing over my shoulder, I saw that it was rather like that day in the cavalry camp. A bunch of doubters, among whom I had at least one well-wisher—Jacob—stood around waiting for me to get to it.

"Okay, Shandy," I said, taking the hackamore rope in a firm grip, and putting words in his ear. "You're a nice little spotted little pretty little pony that wants to behave and not disgrace the two of us in front of all these people, am I right? Course I'm right . . ."

Shandy swung his head around, intending to bite, and got my shirt between his teeth. I ignored a few snickers behind me, and continued to talk softly while leading the horse toward the saddle.

"Now, *stand* like a fine fellow and I'll just get this here saddle on your back—you're used to the saddle by now so don't try to put it over that you're not—you been sacked 'n' saddled to a fare-thee-well . . . *That's* fine, *that's* the way—now jes' keep standin' while I slither up the side of you here—easy, easy easy—nothin' to it—foot in the stirrup . . . You ever hear the one about Mr. Lincoln's hoss, got its foot caught in the stirrup 'n' Mr. Lincoln said to him, 'Paint, if yore gettin' on, I'm gettin' off!' There, I knew you'd think that was funny—quit tryin' to bite, will ya—it looks plumb awful in front of all these people—"

I grasped the pommel, got my foot in the stirrup, swung on up and over.

When he felt me in the saddle—another darned creature on *his back,* and, for all he knew, could be a *mountain lion*—that animal arched his neck, snorted, gave a few little humpy practice jumps, then bucked for the sky and tore around the corral bucking and twisting the way any self-respecting half-broke bronco had a right to do, and I hung on, centered in the saddle but sliding forward, fanning my hat for balance, feet shoved hard in the wooden stirrups, as any self-respecting rider had *his* right to do.

After a seeming hour that lasted perhaps twenty minutes, Shandy (to me) slowed up, finally stood, sides heaving, breath coming in large gusts. I patted his neck, tossed his mane a bit, leaned over and told him a few words from Shenandoah, waiting until, though still flaring his nostrils and snorting, he got quieter.

Finally, holding on to his left ear to keep him from twisting around to bite, I slid out of the saddle, and began to walk him.

"Where'd you learn to ride like that, son?" Ewen Frost asked.

"Virginia," I said, and he didn't pursue the matter, but said instead, "Can you rope?"

"I'm learning, from Jacob."

"You got a good teacher. One-armed, he can rope as good as any man in Texas."

"Cezzy's gonna be that good, too," Jacob said. "Got a knack, he has, with anythin' that's to do with hosses."

Mr. Frost lit a cigarette, blew out a stream of smoke, glanced at the man beside him. "What say, Pete? Shall we take him on?"

"We better, or some other outfit'll get him."

"Okay, son. What's your name again? Cezanne *Pinto?* That's a funny one, all right. Okay, Cezanne, you can go in the roundup with my gang, chuck wagon number four. You're wrangler, take care of the remuda, help Cooky with peeling and washing up and on and on and so forth. Mind, it's not an easy job.

I'll have someone show you the ropes. Ten dollars a month. If you work out, fifteen per on the drive."

Oh oh oh! To be that happy! I wanted to buck like a bronco, right to the ceiling of sky.

A lot of the hands were grinning at me—partly, I suppose, pleased to see anyone getting such a kick out of the chance to ride drag in a cloud of dust for fifteen bucks a month, and partly knowing what I was in for.

Old hands get a kick out of greenhorns.

Mr. Frost and Jacob settled that in return for getting valuable me, his men would keep an eye out for the BoxK brand on the cattle they brought in.

"I figger there's four, five hundred, Ewen. Mebbe even more. Iffen you'd run mine to Wichita with yourn, you kin take half what they bring. That sound fair?"

Ewen Frost allowed as how that would be fair.

Several weeks later, going north on the Chisholm Trail to the railhead at Wichita, Kansas, I learned what the grinning had been about. The wrangler was always the youngest, newest recruit. He rode, bandanna over his nose, in a constant cloud of dust and smells sent back by a mile-long column of grazing and bellowing cattle that preferred not to be hurried, and the shouting whistling cowboys herding them, keeping them in line and on the move, not too fast but steady.

Even on days when nothing went wrong, when the trail boss, riding well ahead, had found us good bed ground—that is, an area flat enough, grassy enough, with sufficient water so that the cattle would settle without complaint—even then the work was constant. There were always critters making a break for it that had to be rounded up and inserted back into the line. There were rivers to ford, sometimes so swollen that hours were spent persuading the herd to make the crossing, and it was not unknown for some of them to drown, even for a cowboy to drown in the mass confusion. And then, we never knew when some spooky Longhorn, alarmed by the shadow of a buzzard passing over, by a distant thunder clap, by a jackrabbit jumping across the trail, would set off a stampede. A stampede could be anything from a false start easily diverted, to a raging horde of Longhorns prepared to run down anything in its path.

On a night when the herd, having been turned off the trail to eat and drink, was resting quietly, I sat by the campfire working on a letter I'd been writing for several weeks, to Tamar and the Ramseys. Besides a book, and Cupid's mouth organ, I carried pencil and writing pad with me always. It's the second letter Mrs. Ramsey sent to me, long after the events were past, to let me include it in my "memoir."

Dear Tamar and Mrs. and Mr. Ramsey: It's way past sundown and things are pretty quiet. The night riders are circling the herd, singing to it. That's interesting, isn't it? Longhorns like to be lullabied to sleep, and I don't know a cowboy who can't either sing or anyway whistle good. It's lovely to hear them out there in the dark. What isn't lovely to hear is what I—I mean all of us—heard a few nights ago, and that's a kind of rumble in the ground that means a stampede may be boiling up. These great big animals are brave as can be, and also so scary you wldn't believe. Any little thing and the whole herd is off and running with hooves like thunder

263

and they can weigh 5 to 800 lbs so thousands of them running and you somewhere in the middle is a dreadful, dire situation. That night all hands except me and Cooky— we got under the wagon, a stampede will just abt always swing around a wagon, not go through it—were out of their bedrolls and onto their horses in minutes. The swing and point riders, usually the best men on the fastest horses, gallop like mad to catch up with the lead steers to turn them back and wind the herd into a wheel, going round and round hooting and hollering till the animals get tired, just milling around and around till they figure its time to settle again. Times, a stampede can keep up for ages and scatter over miles so that the men have to spend hours, even a day or so, rounding them all up and getting them back in a line moving forward. The one the other night was what you might call a semi-stampede. Came to nothing but a short chase, thanks be. But I wonder if I'm cut out for this life. I love anything to do with a horse but the way these fellows go galloping across the prairie after cattle that're trying to escape in a pitch black night not paying a mind to chuck holes or ditches, needs a kind of craziness—and braveness, too—that I'm not sure I have. And beside—I couldn't tell anybody here this— but I have this kind of *liking* for the cows. (That's any cattle, steers included, I guess I already told you.) Anyway, Longhorns have a kind of strength and pride that sometimes makes me ashamed to be doing this to them, and the branding is *awful*. But then I remember that I have to work somehow, and this way I can be with horses all the time, and I like most of the people too. Well, so I guess I wont quit. I told you in another letter abt the horse, Shandy, that I first rode for Mr. Frost. They took him on, but of course not for me. He's in the remuda (I've told you what that is) with Pete Wilson's five other horses and Pete likes him best of all. I've got a nice old quarter horse, Bebe, who can cover the distance when asked. I still am on drag, bringing up stragglers, I've learned to rope pretty good, and of course trying to get along with Cooky. I want to tell you, Cooks are just abt more important than trail bosses in this life, and it's dumb to get on the wrong side of one. There's a funny story they tell about a tenderfoot who made a face when he bit into some cook's sourdough biscuit. The cook stomped over and said, "Sumpin' wrong with that there biscuit?" And the poor young cowboy said, "It's burnt on the bottom, it's burnt on the top, it's raw in the middle an' it tastes like a salt mine. *Just* the way I like 'em, Cooky!" Well, me for the bedroll. Have to be up at dawn to bring in the remuda. The sky is spangled with stars, no moon. The night riders are still singing while they go round and round the herd, and they're making me sleepy, too. Do you know this song? *Oh remember the Red River Vallee and the cowboy that loved you so true* . . . There's a coyote barking out there mixed up with the boys singing and it all sounds so sad and lonely and sweet, in the darkness. Give my love to Majolie. I been writing this for weeks and hope it finds you all well and happy. Remembering you, always and always, Cezanne.

During those years in Texas and on the trail, mail from Clive Court was inexpressibly dear to me. I tried to keep all of it safe, to read and reread, but storms and stampedes, fatigue and carelessness cost me some of the precious letters, and I still regret every one lost.

A long message from Tamar disappeared. She wrote that she was teaching in the Chicago public schools after earning her degree from a teachers college in Normal, Illinois. (Teachers colleges everywhere were called normal schools. After that town, I suppose. Normal is part of Bloomington today—another odd floating fact that will not leave my mind.)

Those so-called teachers colleges hadn't the academic standards of today. Perhaps they couldn't rightly be called standards at all. Children went to them right out of the eighth grade, reviewed what they'd already learned, then set out to become teachers themselves. Quality, you'll understand, varied wildly.

Of course, Tamar became a teacher to pattern by.

She conceded, in that letter or another, that she realized one could not be a guide, a tutor to the young, with only the Bible for resource, though that resource was always, for her, first and unequaled. Nonetheless, she had become a reader of not only Dickens but vast numbers of writers. Novelists, poets, historians. She'd always been clever about arithmetic, and had added mathematics and some science to her store of knowledge. So as, she said, to be a worthy mentor to children.

Oh, yes . . . what Tamar undertook to do was done with the golden touch—not of money, but of diligence and determination, of wisdom and common sense, of hard hard work. What she offered, to those who would take, was riches. She had disciples who admired and imitated her. Not many, I fear, loved her. That strict high-mindedness was daunting to all but a few. I count it the most fortunate circumstance of my life that I was one of the very few for whom she would lower her shield of rectitude in order simply to *play*. That I, in truth, was the first person in *her* life from the time we ran off together until the day she followed Jim Maury and so many others down that long tunnel.

*   *   *

Well, back to Texas and the trail.

In time, finding in myself the necessary craziness, or courage, to take off in the dark after a bolting cow, not worrying about chuckholes and ditches, I became a swing rider. I had learned just fine how to throw a rope. Could pick my horse out of the remuda from thirty feet away, catch a critter by the horns while galloping full speed after him.

There it was, and there the years went.

I rode with the RollingQ for five years, trailing up the Chisholm to Wichita. Sometime in there I met up with Mr. Charles Goodnight, who offered me a job. His drives went up the Goodnight-Loving Trail all the way to Montana, and the idea of a different, riskier route, with a chance to see more of the world, was tempting. Besides, his top hand was a black man, Bose Ikard. Bose was a famous rider, and I'd have given plenty to get to know him.

But.

It wasn't only that I'd come to like Ewen, and by then was riding point and considered a top hand myself, getting top wages. Forty dollars a month, most of it saved. There was also the matter of Cal and

Jacob. They were my friends, and I was theirs. You don't leave friends if you can help it. Of course, it often turns out that you don't have a choice, but just then, at that time of my life, I did have a choice.

I stayed.

I never did like bunkhouses full of cowhands passing winter months in braiding lariats, playing cards, riding into town to stir up trouble, lying around grousing, waiting for spring and the next roundup. I spent part of my winters not at the RollingQ but with Cal and Jacob, turning that place back into a going ranch. The BoxK. Didn't rival Ewen Frost's spread, but respectable enough so that in a couple of years we trailed over five hundred head with Ewen's drive.

It was during the first winter that I became a teacher.

Evenings, to pass the time, I'd been reading aloud to Cal and Jacob from *Oliver Twist*. I'd gone ahead in the book, unable to wait to find out what happened, and was just about devastated to find that several chapters at the end were missing. Just as Monks was on his way to the workhouse to see Mr. and Mrs. Bumble, my copy stopped, *mid-sentence*.

Dreadfully cast down by this, not knowing if I'd ever find another copy, I hadn't had the heart yet to tell the Trillo brothers, who hung on every word each evening.

"Must be a treat," Jacob said more than once, "bein' able to make out these words so y'all know what all is meant by them. How'd you larn to do that, Cezzy?"

"From two wonderful women. Tamar and Mrs. Ramsey, they both taught me. There's no way I could ever thank them."

"They wanna be thanked?"

"No. I just wish now that I had thanked them enough."

"Mebbe that you larned is thanks 'nough?"

I smiled. "That's nice, Jacob."

"Ever think on teachin' someone your own self? That'd be a way to pay 'em back, right?"

"It sure would. Do you—" I studied his lean face. "You mean you'd like to learn to read?"

"An' write, the good Lord willin'. I cain't rightly think of anythin' I'd prefer."

"Well, gosh, Jacob . . . that's wonderful! That's marvelous! Look here, I've got a grammar and a dictionary and a couple of books by Dickens, so even if maybe we'll never find out how this one comes out—"

I stopped, put out with myself for blundering.

Cal scowled at me. "What's that mean? We won't know how it comes out? You tellin' me it ain't a real finished book? We ain't gonna fin' out what happens to all them people?" He sounded actually angry. "Why dint you buy a book with a endin' to it? What's the feller doin' anyways, writing a book without no ending?"

"Cal!" I shouted. "The book has an ending. Just our copy doesn't."

"So, how come?"

"You remember how we rushed through New Orleans. I just grabbed this up in that shop. I couldn't read it right there on the spot, now could I? How was I to know the last chapters were missing? I don't like it any better'n you do."

Cal subsided. "Cain't rightly blame you, I s'pose."

"When we gonna start in on my lessons, Cezzy?" Jacob asked impatiently.

"Are we still going to San Antonio tomorrow?" I asked.

"Wal, sure. That's what we planned on. Carmen can look out fer the place fer a coupla days."

(By now, we actually had a housekeeper, a distant cousin of the Trillos. Young, sort of plump, good cook, very very pretty, and took care of things, including us. I was sure Jacob was in love with her, though he gave no outward sign. Perhaps, I decided, he didn't think a man with one arm could give a woman a whole life. She made him understand that he was wrong, but it took a few years.)

"When we're there," I told him, "we can get some notebooks and pencils and we'll find more books to read out loud, while you're learning to read to yourself. I'll betcha we can even find another copy of *Oliver Twist,* one with the ending in." I was getting quite excited at the prospect. "How about you, Cal? You want to study with us too?"

"Count me out. I got this far without bein' eddicated. Guess I'll go right on thataway. I jes' wanna know how Oliver and Nancy and those Bumbles came out."

"Well, if you change your mind—here I am!"

Next day we three were off to San Antonio, originally to order me a pair of handmade boots, but now I was more interested in books and writing materials.

I'd grown two or three inches in the past year, and could no longer wear Carter's teenage shoe leather. I was using a second pair, but the Trillo brothers said that wouldn't do, I had to have my own. I was not reluctant. If a cowboy didn't need them on his feet, he'd wear his boots next to his heart.

We took the Southern Stage, an all-day trip, planning to put up at a hotel where Jacob and Cal and their father had stayed before.

As the day passed, we alternately talked, snoozed, exchanged remarks with the other three passengers. At length we arrived in San Antonio. There I ordered a handsome pair of boots with stitched maple leaves (I had to draw them, as the bootmaker had never seen or even heard of maple trees) from heel to mule-ears. It would take a while to complete the order, so we arranged for me to return in a couple of weeks, and went in search of books. We found an *Oliver Twist* with the complicated end part intact.

When I returned to San Antonio, by myself this time, to collect the boots, I stopped, on impulse, at a daguerreotype studio and there posed in my pride and finery for a "portrait." As it happens, I still have that picture. Adeline, my so loved wife, saved it like an irreplaceable treasure, the way I've saved Jorge Pasquale Trillo's gorgeous boots. Adeline is gone from me, but Majolie, our daughter, saw that no mishap came to picture or boots. Now she's gone too, but here the portrait remains. And the boots.

Oh, *things* are perishable—but not so perishable as people. This house I am writing in is filled with *things* that have outlasted nearly everyone I've loved, though my great-granddaughter, Majolie, loves me despite my age, as I do her, despite her youth.

Sometimes, out of curiosity, or perversity, I study this picture, assuring myself that that boy, standing stiff in front of a painted backdrop of cactus and cloud, so proud in his fancy cowboy duds, was really *I*.

It's fact.

But it *feels* like fancy.

Jacob learned, from me, to read and to write as readily as I had learned, from him, to toss a rope, and it's difficult to say which of us was prouder, and happier—I to have taught him, or he to have learned.

We never tempted Cal as far as the ABC's.

Some of each winter was given to home schooling, besides working to build up the BoxK spread.

But a part of every year I spent on my quest. Cowhands for hundreds of miles around knew how I was looking for my mother, and from all quarters there would come news of a ranch, or private home, or church or school where the cook was a black lady of the right age to be Mam.

At any rumor, I'd saddle up Shandy, whom we'd bought from Ewen Frost, and ride away . . . hoping, hoping to see that dark dear face again. Sometimes I'd be gone for weeks. All across Texas I went searching, into Arizona, New Mexico, once as far as California, and I met a lot of women, dark- or light-complected, good-natured or sour, good cooks or second-rate.

I never found Mam.

No, no, never . . .

Never knew what turn her life took. Never knew how she lived, where or when she died.

I am very old. Therefore sometime long ago Mam must have followed Jim Maury out of this world to the next, to the heaven she *knew* was waiting. Where Tamar, and the Forrests, and the Ramseys must also have gone, since they, too, had perfect confidence in the existence of a celestial home at the top of a flight of golden stairs. I trust it was there when they got to the top. Trust that John Forrest was right in *his* belief that heaven welcomes all, any color, any kind.

I won't be going myself. I think a person has to believe in heaven in order to get there.

This about finishes my memoir.

Too old, too old to go on writing.

Too old, in fact, to go on at all, though I may yet go on awhile. That's in God's hands, or anyway not mine. And I never did plan to record *all* of all my years. Only wanted to speak of when I was a boy. Wanted to put down for anyone, or no one, for *myself*, the tale of the boy I once was.

I wanted to write how it felt to be me . . . slave, runaway, cowboy.

Zora Neale Hurston, that fine writer, entitled an essay "How It Feels to Be Colored Me."

She concluded that, on the whole, it was all right. It was okay to be colored her.

It's okay with me, too, to be colored me.

In my fifth year of trailing, I suddenly—really suddenly—knew it was my last. It was because a Longhorn turned and looked at me.

We were loading our animals onto the freight cars, urging them with cattle prods, when this young steer swung his head around and fixed his dark, hurt-filled eyes on mine.

If you wanted the very model of a perfect Longhorn steer, there he was. Perhaps I remember him that way because he changed my life? He was rangy and long-legged and long-tailed and had a horn spread of sure six feet. He had—I believe I've used the word before about these animals—a noble air. What I shall always remember is that in all that bawling herd—*he didn't make a sound*. He stood, stubbornly refusing the ramp, looking at me. In his gaze was pride and scorn and a dignity that made me swallow hard, and look away, unable to meet his eyes.

Another cowpoke shoved him along into the freight car and I walked off, feeling as Judas might have. I collected my wages that afternoon, wrote to Cal and Jacob, bought a ticket on the Atchison, Topeka, and Santa Fe, and went to Chicago and Tamar.

I went to Chicago, the city founded—if Mam and

legend are to be believed, and I always believed in Mam and in legends—by Jean Baptiste Pointe Du Sable.

I've been here ever since.

Well, as possibly I've said too often, I am now an old man on a siding, and this effort of recalling a past so long past is tiring. Exhilarating, in a way. But— tiring. I shan't need another notebook, since I've said what I had to say.

Thornapple, steeplebush, hawkweed, Queen Anne's lace—that's wild carrot—corn lilies, field pussy-toes, ELECAMPANE!

There now, I believe I'll lie down for a spell . . .

Mary Stolz is the winner of the Kerlan Award for excellence in children's literature and the author of more than fifty books for young readers, including *A Ballad of the Civil War* and the popular *Thomas and Grandfather* series. Her novels *Belling the Tiger* and *The Noonday Friends* were both named Newbery Honor Books. She grew up in New York City and lives in Florida with her husband, Dr. Thomas C. Jaleski.